OSKAR AND THE ICE-PICK

OSKAR AND THE ICE-PICK

by
JUDY CORBALIS

Judy Corbalis.

Illustrations by David Parkins

For Carlo,

with my best

wishes

from Judy

X

ANDRE DEUTSCH

First published in 1988 by
André Deutsch Limited
105–106 Great Russell Street, London WC1B 3LJ

Text copyright © 1988 by Judy Corbalis
Illustrations copyright © 1988 by David Parkins
All rights reserved

British Library Cataloguing in Publication Data

Corbalis, Judy
  Oskar and the icepick.
  I. Title   II. Parkins, David
  823'.914[J]   PZ7

ISBN 0 233 98181 0

Printed in Great Britain by
WBC Print

For:
    Phillip, Toby, Benjamin,
    Dorothy, Alice and Rebecca,

and with thanks to
Margaret and Michael Hathorn.

CHAPTER ONE

Oskar's mother was a famous mountaineer. She was interviewed on radio and television programmes and sometimes she took Oskar to the studios with her. He liked watching what went on and seeing the interviewers talking to his mother.

What he didn't like was being left behind when she went mountain climbing.

"Why do I have to stay with Granny?" he asked.

"Don't let her hear you calling her Granny," warned his mother. "You know she likes you to call her Elspeth. You have to stay with her because you're not old enough to come mountaineering with me yet and you have to go to school."

"But it's the holidays," Oskar pointed out. "And I think I'm old enough to come."

"Well *I* don't and I'm in charge," answered his mother. And that was that.

When she left he went to stay with Elspeth.

Elspeth had been a ballet dancer when she was young. Her house was full of photographs of her in her ballerina's dresses.

"Were you famous?" Oskar had asked her once.

"Very famous," Elspeth had answered, smiling to herself. "Of course, I'm famous now, too, but in a different sort of way."

For, the year before, Elspeth had won the Grandmothers'

Underwater Cross Channel Swimming Race and she had a gold medal from the Queen to prove it.

Oskar sighed. He liked being with Elspeth but it wasn't the same as being with his mother.

"When will Mum be back, this time?" he asked Elspeth.

His grandmother lifted her head out of a bucket of warm water on the kitchen table.

"What, darling?"

"I said, 'When will Mum be back this time?' " repeated Oskar.

"No idea," said Elspeth. "Do you know, I've had my head under water for over three minutes? My lungs are getting stronger every day."

"I don't see why I couldn't have gone with her," said Oskar.

"Too cold, darling," said Elspeth and she stuck her head back in the bucket.

Oskar picked up the cat and went off to watch television. He had just settled down comfortably when the doorbell rang. He got up and opened the door.

A small brown gorilla was standing on the step. The gorilla began to sing in a hoarse voice:

♪♪ *"I'd got up very high,*
Where the ice is thick,
When I found I'd forgotten
My large ice-pick.

I can't go on climbing
Till I've got it again,
So please bring it quickly,
If you can, on a plane." ♪♪

It stopped singing and smiled at Oskar. Oskar looked puzzled.

"Good, wasn't it?" said the gorilla modestly.

"Well, yes." Oskar was doubtful. "But what exactly are you?"

"I'm a special sort of singing telegram," confided the gorilla. "A gorillagram."

"But why are you singing to me?"

"Because of your telegram."

"What telegram?"

"This one, of course," said the gorilla, pulling out a yellow envelope.

Oskar took it and opened it. Inside was a short message. "PLEASE BRING ICEPICK URGENTLY. CORNELIA."

"Cornelia. That's my mother," said Oskar. "But why did she send a gorillagram?"

"I don't know," said the gorilla. "Usually people send them for special occasions."

Elspeth appeared in the hallway. "What a lovely gorilla, Oskar," she cried. "Aren't you going to ask it in?"

"It's a singing telegram gorilla," said Oskar.

"I could sing it again if you like," offered the gorilla.

"No, thank you," said Oskar. He turned to Elspeth. "It's from Mum. She needs her large ice-pick. She left it behind."

"How careless," said Elspeth. "It's probably here in the cellar. I suppose I shall just have to fly out to the Himalayas with it myself."

"It's the holidays. I could come too," said Oskar quickly.

"No, no, darling," said Elspeth. "It's much too far and far too cold. You can go and stay with Uncle Gilbert."

"But I don't like Uncle Gilbert or his house," wailed Oskar. "He never talks to me."

"Never mind," said Elspeth. "I shan't be gone long."

Oskar felt very miserable. A tear slid down his cheek.

"Well, I must be off now," said the gorilla. ♪♪ "Goodbyeeee, Goodbye ee ee," ♪♪ and it danced away down the steps.

Oskar trailed into the kitchen and sat down on the cat.

"OW!!!" screeched the cat.

"I'm not sorry," said Oskar nastily. "In fact, I'm glad."

"You mean thing," hissed the cat and stalked off outside.

Oskar went to bed in a rage. "It's not fair," he complained to himself. "They're allowed to do anything they want and I have to stay here or with Uncle Gilbert. I hate them."

He woke up next morning still feeling very cross.

The sun was shining. "I wish it was raining," he muttered and stamped downstairs to breakfast.

"I'm not going out to play today," he announced to Elspeth and the cat.

"All right, darling," said Elspeth amiably. "Not if you don't want to."

Oskar felt even more annoyed. He wanted her to be cross with him.

"Here," said Elspeth, "a toasted currant bun just for you."

"I don't want it," said Oskar.

The doorbell rang.

"Will you go, please, Oskar?"

Oskar sighed, got up and shuffled to the front door. He opened it. There stood the gorilla.

"Hullo, again," it said. "This time it's for the Grandmothers' Underwater Cross Channel Swimming Champion."

"That's my grandmother. I'll go and get her," said Oskar.

But Elspeth had already appeared in the hallway. "Good heavens!" she cried. "It's that gorilla again! Do come in."

The gorilla stepped into the hall. "I'm not a *real* gorilla," it explained. "I'm actually a person in a gorilla suit. And I've got another telegram for you."

CHAPTER TWO

The gorilla cleared its throat. ♪♪ "La, la, la, la," ♪♪ it began,
then:

> ♪♪ *"I have an invitation*
> *For a swimming race,*
> *And in just two days*
> *It will be taking place.*
> *The Queen has asked especially*
> *If you'll please compete*
> *In the new Grandmothers' Cross-Atlantic*
> *Underwater Feat.*
>
> *We'll pay all your expenses*
> *From the time you start*
> *And we'll fly you back on Concorde*
> *If you do take part,*
> *And we'll send your luggage over*
> *While you're on your way,*
> *But you'll have to get to Liverpool*
> *By twelve o'clock today."* ♪♪

"Good heavens!" cried Elspeth. "I don't believe it! What an
honour! Imagine being personally asked by the Queen to take
part in the Grandmothers' Underwater Cross-Atlantic Race.

Thank goodness I've been in training! How kind of you to bring the telegram."

She patted the gorilla warmly on the shoulder. "Here, have a currant bun. Oskar doesn't want it."

"I do now," said Oskar. But it was too late. The gorilla had eaten it.

"You can't swim to America, Elspeth," said Oskar.

"Of course I can," said Elspeth.

"But you can't!"

"Why not?"

"Because you have to deliver the ice-pick," reminded Oskar.

"Oh dear, I'd completely forgotten it," said Elspeth. "But I can't possibly miss the race. It's so marvellous to be asked to swim. Just imagine how the Queen would feel if she heard I'd refused."

"I don't suppose you'd have such a thing as a cup of tea, would you?" enquired the gorilla.

Elspeth poured out a cup. She looked hard at Oskar. "Excuse me a minute," she said and left the room.

She came back carrying the ice-pick. "It *was* in the cellar," she said. "Now, Oskar, just lift this up."

Oskar lifted the pick. It wasn't heavy at all.

Elspeth looked hard at him again. "I have a surprise for you," she said. "*You* are taking the ice-pick to your mother. *I* am going to Liverpool to race."

Oskar's face went bright pink with excitement. His heart thumped madly. He couldn't believe it. At last he was going somewhere.

The gorilla had finished the tea. "Thank you. That was just what I needed," it said, "and now, I must be off."

"Just a moment," said Elspeth. "I want to send a telegram."

The gorilla sat down again. "I hope it's easy," it sighed. "I have such trouble making rhymes."

"Very easy," answered Elspeth. "It's just one line. It says, "AM SENDING OSKAR AND THE ICE-PICK. ELSPETH.""

"I can't make a song out of *that*," objected the gorilla.

"You don't have to," said Elspeth. "It can be just an ordinary telegram. As long as it gets there."

"Where?"

"The Himalayas."

"The Himalayas. Where on earth are they?"

"They're a huge mountain range in Nepal, near China," explained Elspeth.

"I'm not sure we've got an office there," said the gorilla.

"You must have," said Elspeth, "or she couldn't have sent one to us."

"True," said the gorilla. "Well, I'll take it back with me now."

"And you, Oskar," said Elspeth, "have to pack your things *very* quickly. We haven't much time."

Within an hour Elspeth, Oskar and the ice-pick were in a taxi and on their way to the airport.

"The Himalayas are very cold," said Elspeth. "You must remember to wear your gloves once you're there. You don't want to get frostbite. I'll give you some money now to last you until you see your mother."

Oskar hugged the ice-pick very tightly. "How will I find Mum?" he asked.

"Oh, easily," said Elspeth. "She'll be camped at the foot of the mountains somewhere. Simply ask at the airport. Anyway, they'll be expecting you. I've sent the telegram."

"Look!" Oskar pointed out of the window.

There was the gorilla riding by on a bicycle.

"Hullo!" shouted Oskar through the glass.

The gorilla waved and the bicycle wobbled dangerously.

"Such a sweet animal," said Elspeth, "but not a very good bicycle rider." She was wearing her aqua-lung in the taxi. "I must get accustomed to the weight," she explained.

They arrived at the airport. Oskar picked up the ice-pick and kissed Elspeth.

"Wish me luck!" cried Elspeth. "By the time you return, I may have become even more famous. I do hope I win. I think I might."

"Good luck, Elspeth," said Oskar. She kissed him, waved goodbye and was off. Clutching the ice-pick, Oskar walked towards the airport entrance.

"You can't bring that ice-pick in here," said the official at the door.

"It's baggage," said Oskar. "I'm going to the Himalayas."

The official let him pass.

Oskar checked-in his suitcase.

"You'll have to carry that ice-pick," said the man at the desk. Oskar went through passport control and into the departure lounge. He looked at the flight times. His plane was boarding already so he set off down a long corridor to the departure gate where he joined a queue of passengers. After a while the queue began to move and finally Oskar was inside. He put the ice-pick into the luggage compartment above his seat, sat down and had just done up his seatbelt when there was a commotion at the door.

"You can't come aboard!" someone was shouting.

And a familiar voice cried excitedly, "I tell you I *can* come aboard. I've got a proper ticket. I'm not an animal; I'm a person in a gorilla suit. I'm a gorillagram and I'm delivering an urgent message."

"I've never heard of a gorillagram," said the first voice.

And the second voice said impatiently, "It's a sort of singing telegram."

Oskar undid his seat belt, jumped up and ran down the aisle.

"It's all right," he said to the air hostess. "It's quite safe: I know that gorilla. It's a friend of mine."

"Fancy seeing you here!" said the gorilla. "I'm on my way with your grandmother's telegram."

"But I'm on the way too," said Oskar. "And the telegram was supposed to get there *before* me so they knew I was coming! What shall I do?"

CHAPTER THREE

"You can't do anything. The plane's nearly leaving," said the gorilla.

"But why didn't they send it to someone there to deliver? They must have an office in the Himalayas," said Oskar.

"They have, but they can't get through to it," explained the gorilla. "The person in the office doesn't seem to be there so they've had to fly me out."

"But why can't it be just an ordinary telegram?" asked Oskar.

"It's a brand-new service from the Post Office. *I* only found out about it yesterday. Everyone has to have telegrams sung to them now. And frankly," the gorilla went on, "I'm delighted to have a little holiday away. It gets very hot and stuffy riding round on that bicycle in a gorilla suit."

"Don't you ever take it off?" Oskar was curious.

"Well, no," said the gorilla, "because I'm an orphan and I'm very poor. I've only got one set of clothes and I'm trying to save them. We don't get paid much and it costs a lot to run the bicycle."

"What do you eat?"

"Exactly the same food as you do," said the gorilla. "Except that when I'm on duty, I'm only allowed bananas."

"I don't think they'll have bananas in the Himalayas," said Oskar.

"Perhaps, as it's cold," said the gorilla hopefully, "they'll have ice-cream instead. Last night and the week before, I tried to buy ice-cream for a treat but both times the shop didn't have any."

"That's funny," said Oskar. "My mother tried to get ice-cream last week too and our supermarket didn't have any. And Elspeth tried to get some at the corner shop yesterday for us but they didn't have it either."

"Do you think they'll have it in the Himalayas?" asked the gorilla.

"Maybe," said Oskar. "Anyway, my mother's sure to know. What's your name? Mine's Oskar."

"I'm Henrietta," said the gorilla. "How old are you. I'm eleven."

"I'm nine and a half," said Oskar.

"I say," said the gorilla, "where's your grandmother?"

"She's gone off to swim in that competition," said Oskar.

The gorilla was impressed. "I hope she wins," she said. "Well, I'm going to have a sleep now and I suggest you do the same."

They lay back in their seats and slept until the plane landed.

The other passengers, who had watched two films and eaten three meals while Oskar and Henrietta had been asleep, got up and started to disembark.

"You two are to stay on board," said the air hostess. "The plane makes one more stop closer to the mountains and that's where you get off."

The engines revved up and they took off again. Oskar peered out of the window. Huge mountains covered with snow were all around them. "Look," he said to Henrietta.

The gorilla shivered. "I've got a thermal underwear suit

underneath my gorilla costume but it looks *very* cold," she muttered.

"It's cold because it's so high up," said Oskar.

"I don't like the idea of walking in all that snow," sighed Henrietta. "And it does seem a bit silly to be delivering a singing telegram at the same time as the person it's announcing is arriving. I haven't even rhymed it yet. Oh dear."

Oskar squeezed her paw. "I'll help you," he offered. "I'm really glad you're here. It might be quite scarey if I was all by myself."

"But your mother's here," said Henrietta.

"I know," said Oskar, "but I don't know where and those mountains look really big and cold, so it's nice to have you with me."

Henrietta was pleased. She pulled Elspeth's note out of her sleeve.

"AM SENDING OSKAR AND THE ICE-PICK. ELSPETH." she read. "Now how can I make a rhyme out of that?"

"What about this?" said Oskar.

"Look down the mountain.
Quick, quick, quick!
Here comes Oskar
With your large ice-pick."

"That's very good," said Henrietta. "It really is. And it means it's all right for me to be singing it at the same time as you're actually arriving."

There was a sudden bump and a lurch. The air hostess reappeared. "We're just about to land," she said, "so buckle up your seatbelts and put your warm clothes on. It's cold out there."

Outside the windows everything was brilliant white. Deep snow lay over the mountains but the sky was blue and clear. The engines slowed and the plane touched down. Oskar and Henrietta got ready to get off.

"Don't forget your ice-pick," reminded the air hostess.

The door opened and they went down the steps onto the airport landing strip. But it wasn't a proper airport at all!

CHAPTER FOUR

They looked around them. There was nothing except a strip of tarmac with a small weatherboard hut nearby and enormous towering snow-capped mountains. They heard a loud roar from behind them as the plane took off again.

"Mum might be waiting there," said Oskar. "Gosh, it's cold."

They trudged across the snow to the hut. There was nobody in it.

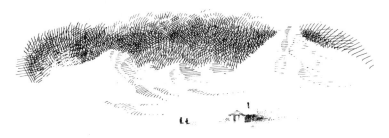

"Halloo-oo-oo-oo!" called Henrietta. Her breath came out in frosty clouds. No one answered.

"It's very strange," said Oskar. "I feel a bit scared. How am I going to find Mum?"

Henrietta looked round. "I shouldn't worry just yet," she said. "Perhaps it's lunchtime or something. Or maybe the man in the hut has gone off to fetch your mother."

"But there's nothing anywhere," cried Oskar, and he looked despairingly at the mountains peaking up into the bright blue sky. Everything was dazzlingly white. And it was cold!

"I don't know about you," said Henrietta, "but I'm hungry. And we haven't got anything to eat."

Oskar shivered. "I wish Elspeth had come too," he said.

"I expect she's in Liverpool by now," said Henrietta.

"Yes," replied Oskar, thinking enviously of Elspeth in her rubber swimming costume. "I'll bet she is, too. With lots of people round, and food and . . ."

"Stop it," said Henrietta. "You're making me feel hungrier. Let's go into the hut. Maybe there's some food in there."

Inside, the hut was very simply furnished. The walls were made of dried mud and someone had tacked coloured pieces of cloth on them. There were two chairs, a long table covered with pieces of official-looking paper, a wooden cupboard, and a shelf in one corner and a broom in another. Behind the door hung a woolly sheepskin coat and a felt hat with long earflaps lined with fur.

"Look!" cried Henrietta, pointing to an old fashioned iron stove with a chimney going out through the roof. Beside the stove was a large basket full of logs. She knelt down, opened the door of the stove and peered in. The fire was still alight but was dying down. She blew on the embers, took a log from the basket and was just putting it on, when there was a noise from behind her, and a shrill scream and a thump as somebody shut the door from the outside.

"Maybe you shouldn't have touched the fire," said Oskar.

"Well, let's go after whoever it is," said Henrietta, "and explain we've just arrived and we're very cold."

She opened the door. A small squat man was peering nervously round the side of the hut. When he saw Henrietta, he gave another shrill shriek and disappeared. She set off after him.

"Henrietta! Stop!" cried Oskar. "He thinks you're a gorilla."

"Oh dear," said Henrietta. "I completely forgot I had my suit on. I get so used to it, you see."

"Wait here," said Oskar. "I'll go," and he stepped outside into the raw fresh air.

"Hullo!" he called.

There was no answer.

He walked round the hut, following the deep footprints in the snow. There was no sign of the man but the footprints led on over a snowy ridge behind the building and away into the distance.

Oskar went back into the hut. "He's gone," he said to Henrietta, "and I don't think we'll find him for quite a while. The trouble is you look exactly like a gorilla."

"I can't help that," snapped Henrietta. "I wish I'd never come. I don't see how we're ever going to find your mother and I wish I was back at home riding my bicycle. I'm frozen and hungry and we can't find anyone to help and there aren't any shops and the firewood's going to run out soon. *And* I'm supposed to be on duty and working. This is ridiculous."

"Don't go on and on," said Oskar. "I can't help it and it's no use getting cross with me. I thought delivering the ice-pick would be easy. I had no idea there were so many mountains and I don't know which one Mum's camped on or anything."

"All right," said Henrietta, "I didn't mean to be nasty. It's just a bit different from the way I thought it would be. Don't worry, I'm sure we'll find your mother. I mean, there can't be many foreigners around so we'll probably just have to ask."

"But there's no one *to* ask," said Oskar.

"We'll find someone," said Henrietta. "If we follow those footprints, we'll probably find your mother in the next few hours."

"Do you think so?"

"Yes, I do," said Henrietta. "Now, let's put more wood on the fire and get a bit warmer."

They stoked it up and knelt closer.

"That's better," said Oskar.

"Don't move or look round," said Henrietta very quietly, "but there's someone outside the window, I think."

Oskar shivered. He moved his head slightly but he couldn't see anything.

Suddenly, the door burst open! There stood six men dressed in sheepskin coats, holding large pointed sticks.

The tallest one stepped forward. "Come with us," he said. "We have orders to bring you. Come at once or we will beat you with these sticks."

CHAPTER FIVE

"We'd better do as he says," muttered Henrietta. "Don't forget the ice-pick."

They got to their feet and walked slowly to the door. The men clutched their sharp sticks but kept well away from Henrietta.

"I'm sure they think you're a gorilla and they're a bit scared," whispered Oskar. "Make sure they don't hear you talking to me."

Henrietta pulled an ugly face and jumped up and down.

"Chee! Chee, chee, chatter, gibber, gibber, chee!" she called.

The men backed away nervously.

"Come on!" said the smallest one. "Over here." And he pointed to the ridge where the footprints went.

Oskar thought that perhaps they were going to follow the footprints till they reached the airport official. And if that was the case, then he could try to find out where his mother was. Maybe these men were not as nasty as they seemed. After all, Henrietta did look like a gorilla. He decided to try to talk to one of them.

"I'm looking for my mother," he said. "I want to find my mother."

The man looked blank. Oskar pointed to the ice-pick.

"It's an ice-pick," he tried again. "For my mother."

"Give it to me," said the man, and he tried to wrest it away.

"No!" cried Oskar and clung to it. The man let go.

"Oskar," whispered Henrietta, "I shouldn't draw their attention to it if I were you. I don't think they're very friendly."

"I thought they might know where Mum is," explained Oskar.

"I know," said Henrietta, "but I don't think they would tell you, even if they knew. Let's just see where they're taking us."

The snow was deep and soft in places and the sun shone so brightly onto it that their eyes stung from the glare. Their breath was white and fuzzy and stayed suspended in the air. It was hard work walking. Their feet left great imprints in the snow. They reached the ridge and began climbing slowly up, leg after leg, paw after paw.

"I'm tired," said Oskar.

"And I'm finding it a bit hard to breathe," panted Henrietta. "It must be because we're up so high and the air's thinner."

"It is," said Oskar. "Mum explained it to me once. It's called altitude sickness. It can make you feel really ill."

"I'm starting to feel sick already," said Henrietta. "I've got to sit down soon."

"We're nearly at the top," said Oskar. "I wonder what's on the other side."

They had struggled on for a minute or two when suddenly Henrietta whispered, "Look!" They peered over the snow bank.

There, in front of them, far below on the side of a mountain across the valley, stood a huge white palace. The sun caught its marble domes and made them glitter and shine. Its tall spires stood out against the sky and its windows sparkled in the light.

"It's beautiful," breathed Oskar. "You see, these men aren't so bad after all. That must be where they're taking us. Someone very important must live in that palace. They're sure to know where my mother is."

"But we've got to get there first," pointed out Henrietta. "It's a long way away and we're tired already. I can't walk anymore."

And she sat down in the snow.

"Get up!" called one of the men.

"She can't," said Oskar. Henrietta went on sitting.

"*Get up*!" cried the man again.

"No! No! No! No! No!" shouted Oskar as Henrietta began to wave her arms around wildly. "She's TOO TIRED!"

His legs had started to ache and his chest hurt. He sank down into the snow too. From under his sheepskin coat, one of the men produced a rolled-up animal skin. He undid it, laid it down and pointed to it.

"I think he means us to sit on it," said Henrietta getting to her feet. "Come on," she whispered to Oskar. The skin felt quite dry and warm but it smelt salty. His nostrils tickled.

"Pooh! It smells like cheese,' muttered Henrietta. Oskar wrinkled his nose.

"I don't like it either," he said, "but I'm so tired and it's the only thing around here to sit on."

They settled themselves in the middle, then each of the men took a corner and began to pull. The skin slipped quite easily downhill over the snow and, in a short time, they were at the bottom in the valley.

"Oohh!" said Henrietta, "I enjoyed that. It was a bit like sledging."

"Have you got a sledge?" asked Oskar.

"No, not now," said Henrietta slowly. "But I used to have one."

"Mine's great." said Oskar. "It's made of wood and you put wax on the runners. It used to belong to my Uncle Gilbert. What was yours like?"

"Oh, SHUT UP!" said Henrietta angrily. "And mind your own business. Just stop pushing your nose into my affairs. It's nothing to do with you what my sledge was like."

Oskar felt hurt. "Henrietta's mean," he thought. "And nasty. I wish she hadn't come. You can't say anything without her flying off the handle and being rude. She's just bad tempered and stupid." He swallowed hard and blinked his eyes. Here he was, without his family, in a strange country, with a heavy ice-pick which he was sick of lugging around. He thought angrily of Elspeth and how she had told him it would be easy to find his mother. "Just ask at the airport," she'd said.

"But there wasn't anyone to ask at the airport," he said to himself. "There wasn't even an airport."

He blinked again.

"Are you crying?" asked Henrietta.

"No," said Oskar shortly.

"You are," said Henrietta.

"I am NOT," cried Oskar. "Leave me alone!"

Meanwhile, the men had been busily occupied in talking to one another and digging into various bags. They began to pull out food which they placed on a cloth laid on the snow. Then they all started to eat. Oskar looked at the food and his mouth

31

watered. It didn't look much like the food he was used to but he suddenly realised how hungry he was.

One of the men handed him a bowl with steam rising from it. Oskar looked at it dubiously.

"Go on," hissed Henrietta. "Try it."

Oskar glanced at her coldly and turned away. The bowl seemed to have tea in it with little beads of fat swimming on the top.

Another man handed a bowl to Henrietta. As soon as he was out of earshot, she smelt it, and blew on it to cool it, then took a tiny sip.

"Ooh," she snorted, "it's disgusting. But I'm so hungry, I'm going to drink it."

Oskar ignored her. He didn't want to be friends any more now.

"What do *you* think of it?" asked Henrietta.

Oskar said nothing. Henrietta leaned over and patted his shoulder.

"You're sulking," she said.

"Oh, shut UP!" cried Oskar.

"It's me," said Henrietta. "I know I was rude to you, and I'm sorry, but I couldn't help it."

"You're always being nasty to me," said Oskar, "and I'm sick of it."

"I am sorry, truly I am," said Henrietta. "Please be friends again. I didn't mean it. Look! You can see the palace much more clearly now. It's just like a fairy castle."

Oskar blew on his tea to cool it. "If you're nasty like that again, I won't be friends," he said.

"I'll be nice," said Henrietta. "I promise. Now try this tea stuff. It tastes really greasy but it's warm."

Oskar took a large swallow, choked and spluttered. Then he started to laugh.

"That's better," said Henrietta. "You know, I can't believe they really have a telegraph service here. There aren't any people around."

"Maybe there's a king in that palace."

"Or a queen," said Henrietta. "But even so they couldn't send enough telegrams to have a whole office to themselves."

"Perhaps they're very rich," said Oskar, "so they *do* have a whole office to themselves and that's where you're supposed to be delivering Mum's telegram. That's probably why they've come to get us. Maybe Mum's waiting there now."

Henrietta felt it was very unlikely but she decided to say nothing. She looked over towards the palace again.

"Look over there," she said. "The snow's moving."

"Moving?" said Oskar. "It can't be. Don't be silly."

"I'm not being silly," said Henrietta. "See for yourself."

Oskar peered across the valley to where she was pointing.

"It *is* moving," he said. "But that's impossible. Do you think it's an avalanche?"

"Avalanches don't go sideways," said Henrietta. "Anyhow, it's not just one piece of snow, there are lots of bits of snow moving."

Oskar got up and went over to the guards.

"See," he said and pointed. There was a moment's silence, then pandemonium broke out. Tossing their bags and bowls into the snow, the men raced off screaming, leaving Oskar and Henrietta sitting on the skin.

"Hey!" cried Oskar.

"Wait for us!" called Henrietta.

But it was no use. The men were running off towards the ridge they had just crossed.

"Oskar," said Henrietta, "that moving snow's come a lot closer. Only it's not snow. Definitely not. Have another look. Do you see what I see?"

CHAPTER SIX

Oskar peered across at the moving snow. "Oh no!" he cried. "It's a whole lot of wild animals!"

"That's what I thought, too," said Henrietta in dismay. "They're very big and white and woolly. Do you know what they are?"

"They look a bit like monkeys to me," said Oskar. "But they couldn't be: they're too big and they're white."

"They're not monkeys," said Henrietta. "I know what they are – they're yetis."

"YETIS!" shrieked Oskar. "Yetis are dangerous! They eat people! They're called abominable snowmen! My mother told me about them, but she said they didn't actually exist."

"Well, it looks as if they *do* exist," said Henrietta. "And they're getting closer all the time."

"But what are we going to DO?" cried Oskar.

Henrietta looked round calmly. "There isn't a lot we can do," she said. "We can't run away because they'd catch us and we can't fight them because they're bigger than we are and there are more of them. And we can't talk to them because they're animals, so what can we do?"

"I could hit them with the ice-pick," suggested Oskar.

"Crazy," said Henrietta. "They'd just take it off you and kill us with it."

"I wish you'd suggest something," said Oskar, "instead of

just saying everything I think of is no good. What do *you* think we should do? And be quick. They're nearly here. And there are an awful lot of them."

There were. Dozens of huge, white, shaggy beasts were lumbering over the snow towards them. The closer they approached, the bigger they seemed.

"Gosh," said Henrietta awed, "they must be at least ten feet tall. All right, I do have a plan. Listen. Whatever happens, our only chance is to look relaxed and casual."

"I don't feel relaxed," said Oskar.

"Nor do I, as a matter of fact," said Henrietta, "but we've got to pretend. You use the ice-pick and I'll scratch out a bit of a hole in the snow and maybe they'll think we're digging for something interesting and they won't take so much notice of us."

Oskar was impressed. "That's brilliant."

"I am quite brilliant," agreed Henrietta. "I often have wonderfully good ideas. It's a shame I haven't got any parents because . . ."

"I'm sorry to interrupt you," said Oskar, "but the yetis are nearly here."

"Oh help," said Henrietta. "Quick, get the ice-pick in position and I'll get on with the hole."

She knelt down on all fours and began scrabbling in the snow. Oskar took the pick, lifted it into the air and swung it down to chip at the icy layer beneath.

"Let's hope it works," he said.

The yetis were coming closer. They moved in a kind of shambling run and, because they were so tall, their long legs covered huge amounts of ground at each stride. They seemed to be of different shapes and sizes, but none of them was less than ten feet tall and they were all almost totally covered in long shaggy white hair and had brownish black eyes set under sloping foreheads. Their leader, a giant of twelve or thirteen feet, was slightly in front and had a baby clinging to her back. As they loped along they communicated with one another in grunts and chattering phrases. Oskar noticed with relief that they didn't seem to have any weapons, but then realised that with such giant paws they probably didn't need them.

The group came nearer. He closed his eyes and clung to the ice-pick. It was very hard to try to look relaxed when any minute now a single swipe might put an end to him.

"Smile!" hissed Henrietta.

"I can't,' said Oskar.

"Go ON!" insisted Henrietta.

Oskar fixed his mouth in a terrible grin. Everything looked even whiter and bluer than it had all day: the palace continued to glitter across the valley as the snow-cloud of yetis came level with them.

Henrietta feigned great interest in the hole. She looked up at the circle of giant animals round her and pointed enthusiastically down it.

"Treasure," she said, and stood up.

Almost immediately, great cries and chatters burst out from the yetis. The leader began grunting and whistling.

Henrietta whistled and grunted back. Oskar, who had continued to clutch the ice-pick, decided it might be sensible to try to dig down into the ice a bit further. Henrietta's idea seemed to be working, at least for the moment, so they might as well prolong it. He took a sidelong look at the nearest yeti and shuddered.

"What is it?" asked Henrietta.

"They're awfully big."

"I know," said Henrietta. "It's a bit worrying."

"I'm going to dig again," said Oskar.

Henrietta moved to one side as he raised the pick.

Instantly, it was snatched from his grasp by a yeti. Oskar grabbed at it.

"Give it back!" he shouted. "It's my mother's!"

Huge hairy arms seized him around the chest, another yeti grabbed Henrietta, and they set off back across the snow again towards the palace.

Oskar's heart was pounding. His nose was pressed into a dense mass of yeti hair so he couldn't see anything but he was conscious of moving at great speed across country. He sneezed, and his captor changed his position so he could see in front of him. They were crossing the snow at a furious pace, and all around, yetis were chattering and gibbering to one another. He caught sight of Henrietta clutched in the arms of the biggest yeti with the baby clinging to her back. Because they were travelling so fast, they were already approaching the palace, and it seemed to Oskar that this must be where they were being taken. But when they were almost at the gates, the group swung suddenly off to the right and away up over the next ridge. Oskar could no longer see Henrietta amidst the throng of white bodies.

Then, suddenly, all the yetis stopped. One minute they were running at speed over the snow, the next they stood stock still. Oskar looked again for Henrietta and this time saw her in the distance. She seemed to have settled down comfortably in her captor's arms and was peering around her.

"Oskar!" she shouted, catching sight of him. Oskar tugged at

his yeti's hair and pointed towards Henrietta. To his surprise, the animal moved to stand next door to her.

"Thank goodness you're still here. I couldn't see you anywhere," said Henrietta. "Where do you suppose we are and what are they going to do with us?"

"Eat us, maybe," said Oskar gloomily.

"I don't think so," replied Henrietta. "The one who's carrying me seems to like me."

And, indeed, Henrietta's yeti was patting her head and making lip-smacking noises in a very friendly way. The baby leaned over its mother's shoulder and pulled at Henrietta's suit. Henrietta smiled at it. Immediately, the mother handed the baby to Henrietta who took it gingerly.

Meanwhile, two yetis who had gone on ahead came shambling back to the others and a conference seemed to be going on.

"I wish I could tell what they're saying," said Oskar. "Oh! We're starting to move." And away they went again across the snow.

They had been going for about five minutes when the entire group stopped. Oskar glanced down at the ground and turned very pale. In front of him, the snow stopped and a huge dark chasm yawned up. They were on the brink of an enormous precipice! His yeti tightened its grip on him and leapt over the edge!

CHAPTER SEVEN

Oskar's stomach lurched and sickened, and the air flew dizzily past him as they plunged down into the darkness. He closed his eyes so as not to see the ground come up and hit them. There was a soft jolt; he opened his eyes and found he was in a huge cave lit from the top by a circular hole in the roof. He had barely had time to realise he was still alive when, one by one, the other yetis came leaping down into the cave. But he could no longer see Henrietta.

All around him were piles of dried twigs and small branches and, as he watched, he saw a large yeti laying a baby down on one of the piles and realised they were beds. At the far end of the cave was a tall stone chair with a rough table next to it. He thought of Elspeth who, by now, was probably swimming in her race, and she seemed entirely unreal.

He wondered where his mother was and what she was thinking and whether *she* missed *him*. How was he going to find her? He might have to spend the rest of his life in this cave, he might be going to be killed, he might never see Elspeth and his mother and the cat and Uncle Gilbert and his friends at school ever again. If only he'd never set off with the ice-pick in the first place.

And where was the ice-pick? What would his mother say if he told her a yeti had taken it? He'd have to get Henrietta to help him explain. But he didn't know where Henrietta was

either. Perhaps her yeti had slipped or crashed jumping down. He shivered and a nearby yeti, noticing this, put its arm round him protectively. Oskar felt better. It didn't seem likely that an animal kind enough to put an arm round him was planning to eat him. Besides, the yeti smelt very comforting, a bit like a sheepskin rug of Elspeth's he remembered. And it certainly was warm. He snuggled up closer.

"I'm tired!" he thought, surprised. His eyelids slipped down over his eyes and, two seconds later, he was fast asleep against the yeti's chest.

* * *

While he slept, an amazing transformation took place inside the cave. Skins were spread over the floor. Some of the yetis went off and returned with roots, strips of bark, vines and mountain flowers. They seemed to be preparing for something, grunting to each other occasionally as they worked. More yetis came clambering in at the cave mouth carrying strange fruits and berries. Then the leader, still with her baby clinging to her back, jumped up onto the table and gave a strange howling cry.

Immediately everyone fell silent. Oskar, woken from his sleep by the cry, opened his eyes just in time to see eight of the largest animals carrying an enormous white leopard skin towards the tall chair. They flung it loosely over the seat, then, to his utter astonishment, their leader gave another wailing cry, all the assembled yetis wailed back and, reaching under the table, she pulled out the ice-pick.

Everybody now stood up and, following the chief yeti's movements, performed a kind of stamping dance. Oskar watched, amazed, as they beat their enormous paws on the cave floor and finally came to rest crouching in a semi-circle round the table and the chair. The yeti queen then seemed to be giving some kind of speech. She chattered and waved and pointed to her baby, she bent double, stretched up and turned in a full circle whilst the others watched silently, then she gave a long reverberating cry, and in at the cave mouth climbed an old-looking yeti carrying a bundle in his arms. He loped up to the chair, placed the bundle on it, and there, as if enthroned, sat Henrietta in her reddish-brown gorilla suit!

CHAPTER EIGHT

Almost immediately, pandemonium broke loose. Yetis jumped and whooped, baby yetis cried, and flowers and leaves were flung into the air at Henrietta's feet like confetti.

"HENRIETTA!" shouted Oskar racing towards her. "What are you doing?"

The crowd of yetis parted to let him through.

"I'm not doing anything," said Henrietta irritably. "It's them doing it to me. I don't know what it's all about. They took me down a precipice and through a tunnel to a horrible place full of skeletons and they were all shouting and getting very excited. I thought they were probably going to kill me and I couldn't see you anywhere so I decided not to just let them get me and I stood up and told them to take me back to the airport AT ONCE!"

"And did they?" asked Oskar.

"Of course not," said Henrietta. "I'm here, aren't I?"

"Well, what did happen?"

"I don't know," said Henrietta. "That big yeti with the baby grabbed me and took me outside into the snow again. Then she brought me back into the bottom of a chasm and climbed up the sides and into the cave. It was terrifying. I had to cling onto the yeti's fur so tightly my hands still hurt. I don't know how their babies manage to hold on all the time."

"But why have they put you here?" wondered Oskar. "I mean, why you and not me? They haven't bothered much about me at all. I've been asleep so I don't know what's been going on."

Henrietta stood up in order to see over the heads of the taller yetis who were sitting right in front of her. Immediately all the yetis stood up too. Henrietta sat down: they sat down. She raised her right hand. Up went all their right paws. She grunted, they grunted.

Henrietta was delighted.

"They do everything I tell them!" she cried.

"Yes," said Oskar, "except that you can't tell them to do much because you don't speak their language."

"That doesn't matter," said Henrietta.

"See if you can get them to take you back to the palace so we can find out who lives there," said Oskar. "I'll bet you can't make them understand."

"I'll bet I can," said Henrietta, nettled. And she stood up again, pointed to herself, then to the cave entrance, and mimed climbing up the precipice. All the yetis stood up, pointed to themselves, pointed to the cave entrance and mimed climbing up the precipice.

Henrietta sat down and put her head in her hands. So did all the yetis. Oskar started to laugh until tears came to his eyes. None of the yetis moved. Henrietta looked at him.

"What's so funny?" she asked.

"It's you," explained Oskar through his giggles. "I've just realised why they're doing this. You've still got your gorilla suit on, only I'm so used to it, I don't notice it any more."

"Of course I've still got it on. I'd freeze to death without it. *And* I've still got my thermal underwear underneath."

"Well, don't you see?" said Oskar. "They think you're a monkey too. Only you're a different colour from them so they think you're something special. I think they've made you their queen."

Henrietta was thoughtful.

"You're probably right," she agreed. "Why didn't I think of that?"

"You're so used to your gorilla suit," said Oskar. "I only realised when I saw them standing up when you did. One brown monkey and dozens of white ones."

Henrietta started to giggle. At once, all the yetis giggled too.

"It's like a permanent game of Simon Says," she said.

"Do you think you could get us something to eat and drink?" asked Oskar. "I'm really hungry."

Henrietta rubbed her hand on her stomach and pointed down her throat. Then she picked up an imaginary spoon and began to eat out of an imaginary dish. The yetis all copied her acting once again but this time, when she had finished miming, the leader jumped up and chattered to the yetis in the front row.

They scampered off and very soon returned with three large steaming bowls, three spoons and strips of what looked like dried meat, but tasted, as they shortly discovered, exactly like salty rubber. The leader then sat down on the floor next to Oskar and, watched by the other animals, began to eat and drink with them.

"I don't actually like this food but I'm getting used to it," said Oskar.

"I'm so starving I could eat anything," said Henrietta. "You know, these don't look like animals' bowls and spoons. They're a bit like the ones I've got at home."

"I know," agreed Oskar. "We've got some like these too."

"Then there must be a shop here somewhere," said Henrietta, "or else where would the yetis get them? And how do you suppose they get money to buy them?"

"They can't possibly go to shops," said Oskar. "They can't talk and no one would know what they wanted. The shop-keepers would be frightened. I'm sure they don't buy them. And I don't believe there are any shops anywhere near here either."

"I think there might be," persisted Henrietta. "We've only seen a little bit of the country. Maybe if we went over just one more ridge, we'd come to a city, or a big town, at least."

"But there aren't any roads," objected Oskar.

"The snow may have covered them," said Henrietta. "And what about that palace we saw? Someone must live there."

Oskar sighed. "I wish we were there now," he said. "I'm sure they'd help me find Mum."

"Those men were horrible. The yetis are much nicer, I think," said Henrietta. "You know they're called abominable snowmen, well, do you really think they're so ugly? Once you get used to them, they've got rather attractive faces."

"They are a bit fierce-looking at first," said Oskar, "especially their eyes and teeth, but I think they're very kind. My one kept trying to keep me warm."

The yetis still sat watching expectantly.

"I'd better do something interesting. The poor things must be bored stiff," said Henrietta, and she got up and stood on her head.

"I can do ballet," said Oskar. "My grandmother taught me. She used to be a famous ballerina."

"Do some now then," said Henrietta, "and I'll copy you, then they'll copy me."

Oskar stood in the fifth position and slowly extended his right leg. Henrietta stood up, got nearly into the fifth position, tried to extend her leg and fell over. All the yetis fell over.

"Look at them," said Oskar with a grin. "They're laughing, Henrietta."

"Monkeys can't laugh," said Henrietta.

"These ones can," said Oskar.

And they were. Clearly, the yetis were having fun.

For quite some time, Oskar and Henrietta went on entertaining the yetis. Then Oskar began to shiver a little.

"Are you cold?" asked Henrietta.

"A bit," said Oskar. "And it's going to get colder still, later. Do you think you could mime some kind of clothing to put on?"

Henrietta sat down and drew an imaginary cloak round herself.

The yetis began chattering and gibbering then, at a command from the leader, one of them went off and came back with two large woollen snow jackets. The leader got up and placed one round Henrietta's shoulders and the other round Oskar's.

"They're lovely, aren't they?" said Henrietta. "They must have a shop nearby. They couldn't possibly have made these by themselves. They're . . ."

She broke off and looked at Oskar. He had gone very pale and was staring at her strangely.

"What's the matter?"

Oskar said nothing.

"What's wrong?" asked Henrietta.

Oskar continued to stare at her.

"*Please*, Oskar!" said Henrietta. "What is it? Tell me what's happened. You look as if you've just seen a ghost."

"I *have* just seen a ghost," said Oskar slowly. "That jacket you've got on – it doesn't belong to the yetis at all. It's my mother's!"

CHAPTER NINE

"Your *mother's*?" Henrietta was incredulous. "How can it be your mother's?"

"I don't know how it got here," said Oskar unhappily, "but I'm positive it's hers. Feel in the pockets and see if there's anything there."

Henrietta felt in the right-hand pocket and pulled out a small scrap of paper.

"It's the same as your telegram," she said, puzzled. "It says, 'PLEASE BRING ICEPICK URGENTLY. CORNELIA'."

"That's my mother," explained Oskar. "She must have made a note before she sent the telegram."

"Well, where is she?" demanded Henrietta.

Oskar hesitated. "I don't know," he said, "but I've got a horrible feeling the yetis must have killed her."

He wanted to cry but he couldn't produce any tears. He just felt numb and terrible.

"Are you definitely here?" he asked Henrietta. "I mean this isn't a dream or something, is it?"

"I'm sorry," said Henrietta. "I really am. It isn't a dream, and it does look as though something bad's happened to your mother. There are bloodstains on this sleeve and on the front of the coat."

Oskar sat silently. If he'd been with his mother perhaps he could have saved her. Why did she always have to go off like this on expeditions, anyway? Other children had *real* mothers who stayed at home and baked cakes and did the washing and things like that. Suddenly he felt angry with her.

"She's got no right to go off all the time," he exploded to Henrietta. "Why didn't she just stay at home with me?"

"She didn't want to, I suppose," said Henrietta.

"Well, she should have," said Oskar, enraged. He was so cross he felt like hitting someone or breaking something.

"I hate her!" he cried.

"OSKAR!" Henrietta was shocked. "That's a terrible thing to say."

Oskar felt twisted up inside. He wanted to hurt someone. "You don't even have any parents," he said, "so how would you know?"

Henrietta burst into tears.

"I wish I did," she sobbed. "And if I had a mother I wouldn't ever say I hated her, especially when she was dead."

The sight of Henrietta in tears had an amazing effect on the yetis. They crowded round petting her and grunting, then the leader picked her up and began to rock her just as if she were a baby. It was very soothing and Henrietta, exhausted from the day's events, fell asleep in her arms. The yeti laid her down and gently placed the coat over her, then lay down herself and also fell asleep. All the other yetis followed suit. Only Oskar, angry and miserable, remained awake. He looked round at Henrietta and the sleeping yetis and, as he did so, the one who had been looking after him earlier, opened an eye, noticed him, got up and plonked him firmly down in a corner to sleep.

"I won't sleep," thought Oskar. He lay with a cold lump of grief and rage inside him. It must be some terrible mistake about his mother. In the morning, they would find her in one of the smaller caves and then things would be all right. Maybe he should call out to her so that if she was nearby she would know he was there.

"Mum!" he shouted. "Mum!"

No one answered. Several of the yetis stirred in their sleep.

"Mum!" cried Oskar, but everything was silent.

He lay back and closed his eyes.

When he awoke it was still dark. He was dimly aware of movement around him and a lot of silent activity going on.

"I must wake up properly," he thought sleepily. Shapes seemed to be gliding by carrying things but there was no sound at all. "I'm dreaming," thought Oskar and drifted off to sleep again.

Some time later he heard his name called from far away.

"Mum!" he tried to call back, but he was too tired to shout.

"Oskar!" he heard once more.

"I'm definitely dreaming," he decided and slipped back to sleep again.

He had a strange and bothering dream. He was being chased by a huge crocodile which kept snapping its teeth at him and which he kept trying to attack with a pencil sharpener. But every time he tried to sharpen the end of its tail, it would swing round and open its huge jaws at him and then he would have to run for it. If only he could get its tail sharpened to a point, he could flick the end back into the crocodile's chest and stab it. That would stop it chasing him. In his dream, he ran and ran. His legs began to buckle under him: the crocodile was coming closer. Oskar looked back over his shoulder at its face and realised it looked like Miss Willester who had been his teacher last year and whom he hadn't liked at all.

Miss Willester the crocodile opened her mouth and snapped at him even harder.

"Oskar," she breathed. "You haven't done your homework. All your sums are wrong. You are bad and I'm going to eat you up."

Oskar fell onto his hands and knees and crawled along the ground as fast as he could. His chest was heavy, his breathing dry and painful. He tried to call out but not a sound came from his mouth. Miss Willester drew nearer. Her dreadful crocodile teeth were closing upon him. Oskar screamed and woke up!

Where was he? He peered around. Of course! He was in the cave. Daylight streamed in through the hole in the roof. But something seemed to be wrong: there was something missing.

The chair and table had gone and so had the piles of vines and flowers. And what had happened to Henrietta and the yetis? With a shock, he realised they had all left without him as he slept. He was alone in the cave.

CHAPTER TEN

Oskar got up off the pile of skins.

"Henrietta!" he called, but there was no answer. The cave was completely empty. They had all gone off somewhere in the night and taken Henrietta with them. Oskar felt stiff and sore from the previous day's walking and he was very hungry. He shuffled over to the cave entrance and peered out. High above him was the edge of the chasm and below, an almost sheer drop of several hundreds of feet.

He shuddered. He was trapped in the cave. He decided to explore the smaller openings off the back wall and was stooping to pick up two or three pieces of the dried meat that he had spotted on the floor, when he noticed his mother's anorak lying nearby.

"I'm cold," he thought. "I ought to put it on."

As he rolled up the sleeves, he noticed again the bloodstains Henrietta had seen the day before. The yetis must have killed his mother and now they'd taken Henrietta away and would probably kill her too. He had to get help. The palace flashed into his mind. Someone there might be able to do something but he'd have to find his way back to it and, before that, work out how to get out of the cave. Back he went to the entrance and looked out. It was a tremendously sheer drop to the snow below, and he couldn't climb up the rock face above.

"If only I had a rope," he thought. "Or an ice-axe or something."

Then he remembered. Of course! He had his mother's ice-pick! Or had the yetis taken it with them? He went back into the cave. There it was, neatly propped against the wall. Oskar's spirits rose. He rushed over to it, seized it, and raced across the cave floor to the entrance again. Now he must find some rope. But a thorough search of the caves revealed no rope at all.

"Then it has to be something else," thought Oskar. "I could try that pile of vines the yetis brought in with Henrietta's flowers last night. There was lots of it and it seemed to be very tough."

He searched amongst the skins, located the pile of vines and pulled out several of the longest strands. To make sure it would be strong enough, he tried to break a vine with his hands but he couldn't: he tried to twist it and snap it but it just bent: he tried standing on it and grinding his heel on it to crush it but that had no effect either. He even thought of trying to bite through it but decided not to in case it was poisonous. Then he sat down and tried to knot it. It was quite hard but he could manage it.

Oskar took twenty pieces of vine, then spent the next two hours reef-knotting them together until he had a long vine rope. Just to be sure he added another few pieces.

"It's long enough," he said to himself. "I'm ready to try now."

Clutching the ice-pick, he climbed on top of a large boulder at the side of the entrance, raised the ice-pick above his head and, using all his strength, sent it crashing down into the ice just by the cave edge. He clambered down, went over to the pick and swung on it. It stayed firm: it was strongly embedded in the ice. Taking his vine rope, he tied one end securely round the centre of the ice-pick, then wound it over and around the handle and knotted it again. He took a medium sized rock, made a noose in the other end of the rope, placed the rock in it, and pulled it tight. Then he threw the rock out of the entrance and down the precipice. He listened for a thud as it landed but heard nothing. Maybe the snow had muffled it. He hauled the rope and it moved up in his hand. He would have to slide down to the end and hope it wasn't too far from the ground.

Oskar pulled on his gloves. He put up the anorak hood and tightened it, then, looking up at the chink of bright blue sky above him, and down at the dark gap beneath, he took a deep breath, stepped over so that the rope was between his knees and clutched at it. The whole of his weight rested on the rope tied to the ice-pick. Would the ice-pick stay secure? Would the rope hold him? He closed his eyes and swung himself out of the cave-mouth into the depths below.

Whoosh!

Dark walls hurtled past as he slid down, down, down into the chasm. Occasionally, a protruding rock bruised and cut him as he plunged on.

"I must come to the end of the rope soon," he thought and had a twinge of terror as he imagined what would happen if he found he was still dangling thousands of feet above the ground.

It was lucky he was wearing gloves. The vine was green and smooth and his hands slid easily, but because the bottom of the rope was not secure, he kept swinging out and hitting the rock face. As the dark wall loomed over him again, he looked up and saw, miles away above, the blue chink of sky at the top of the precipice. Screwing up his courage, he decided to look down. It

occurred to him that perhaps there would be no way of escape at the bottom: it might be just a rock floor. He opened his eyes, and to his amazement saw below him a glimmer of light. There must be a way out down there somewhere.

Suddenly, he came to the end of the rope! Dangling on it, he saw the bottom of the chasm was still over a hundred feet below.

"I should have made the rope longer," he thought and looked around to see what he could do. A little lower down, the precipice walls became much rougher with rocks sticking out. If only he could get down there, he would be able to climb the rest of the way.

He stretched his right foot as far as he could but it didn't reach. Frantically, he searched the walls for crevices. Nearby were several little outcrops of rocks but they were not really big enough to clutch at. His foot was only just out of reach of the big rock. Maybe he could pull on the rope and stretch it. He jerked and twisted like a fish on a hook and then, without any warning, the vine rope snapped!

Oskar screamed as he plummetted through the air. A great white wave seemed to envelop him and he realised he was no longer moving. He tried to open his eyes but his face was covered with snow. He brushed it off and looked up.

Above him, far away, was a thin strip of blue sky. He had fallen on his back into a pile of deep soft snow. Very carefully he moved his legs, found they were all right and sat up. Just ahead was a large tunnel open at both ends. Snow, blown in by the wind, lay thick on the floor.

Oskar crawled along through the deep powdery mounds. Because the snow was so soft, it took him a long time to get to the end of the tunnel and he was exhausted when he reached it. Tired out, he leaned over the edge to look at the countryside below him, lost his balance and rolled over and over down the hillside to the bottom of the slope.

For the second time in one day, Oskar lay on his back and looked upwards. Because he'd been rolling, everything seemed to be spinning. He looked up and saw a church spire appear and disappear. A church spire? That was impossible. He looked again. Directly above him, the sun shone in the same clear blue sky, and tall spires and an ornate dome were pointing into it. He could hear people shouting. He made one more huge effort and sat up. Men were definitely running towards him. Oskar took a long look round and smiled for the first time. Waves of relief wafted over him. He had rolled down the side of the valley right to the gates of the palace he and Henrietta had seen before the yetis had carried them off.

CHAPTER ELEVEN

Oskar lay back. He could hear the shouts of his rescuers getting closer. He tried to call out to them but he was so shaken, exhausted, and bruised that he collapsed into a dead faint.

When he came to, he was in bed in a room of pink and white marble. It was rather cold but he had warm blankets over him and someone had placed a bowl of soup and a spoon on a table by his bed. Oskar sat up. There was something important he had to remember. What was it? His head ached painfully. He tried to think but his mind had gone blank. He looked at the soup. Feeling very hungry, he picked it up and began to drink it. It was tomato – his favourite – but it had another faint taste of something he couldn't quite identify. Anyway, it was delicious and he drank every drop.

Then, on another table near the door, he noticed a plate of what looked like icecream and wafer biscuits. It must have been left there for him. There was no one else in the room so it must be his. On the other hand, if someone had meant him to eat it, wouldn't they have placed it by the soup?

"I'll just taste it," thought Oskar and he climbed out of bed and stuck his finger in the bowl. It *was* icecream! And it was toffee-flavoured. Oskar stuck his finger in a second time and licked it.

"I'll just have one small spoonful," he decided, "and leave the rest."

He swallowed one, then another, and another until there was very little left in the dish.

"I'd better finish it," he said to himself. "It looks worse with just a bit left."

So he did. It was the best icecream he'd ever tasted. And he felt much better now that he wasn't so hungry. Whoever had rescued him was obviously kind. Soup, icecream, a bed, and warm blankets had all been provided for him. Oskar looked around. It was a funny room though. For a start, there wasn't much furniture, just the bed and two small tables. And then there was only one tiny window with a grating across it, high up in the wall so that not even a very tall man could have seen out of it. The door was huge, heavy and made of dark wood, the floor was marble, with a coloured rug thrown over it and the walls and ceiling were all marble. Oskar thought that it was strange to build a marble palace in a cold climate. He remembered how, when they'd been in Italy once on holiday, his mother had explained that the people there used marble a lot because it kept things cool in the heat.

"Maybe it's because the owner of the palace is enormously rich," thought Oskar.

His mother had said marble was very expensive. She'd said ... His mother! Suddenly he remembered! He didn't *have* a mother any more. He looked down at the anorak he still wore and the bloodstains on it. The yetis had killed his mother and now they'd taken Henrietta. Henrietta! That was it! Of course! He'd been trying to find her! If he had any sense, he wouldn't be sitting here eating and drinking, he'd be getting hold of the kind person who had taken him in and getting help to rescue Henrietta. And he'd better be quick!

He got out of bed again and realised as he did so, that he ached and was stiff and sore all over his body. He limped to the door and tried to turn the handle. It was too big. It wouldn't move. Oskar took it in both hands and twisted it. This time the latch turned but still the door didn't open. He shook it again. It was bolted!

"But why would they lock me in?" he wondered.

Then he supposed that, after all, whoever had rescued him didn't know who he was or what he wanted and it was probably very sensible of them to lock him in till they found out about him.

"But I have to get help to Henrietta," he reminded himself, "so I'd better shout and let them know I'm awake."

He cupped his hands round his mouth.

"Hallo!!" he shouted through the bolted door. "Hallo! Are you there-ere? I'm awake now! Hallo-o!!!"

No one answered. For a moment Oskar felt panic-stricken. Maybe no one would hear him for a very long time.

"What nonsense!" he reassured himself. "It's probably lunch-time or something and they're somewhere else just now."

It occurred to him to wonder what time it really *was*. He took the two tables and placed them on top of each other under the window.

Gingerly, he clambered up onto them but was disappointed to find the window was still too high to peer through. He got down and replaced the tables. Then he took off one of his shoes and banged hard on the door with it.

"Hallo!!!" he called again. "Is anyone around? I'm up!! HALLO!!" But still nobody answered him.

"They'll probably come in a little while," he decided, and lay down on the bed again.

Just as he was drifting back to sleep, he thought he heard voices. Quickly he got up, smoothed the blankets and brushed his hair with his fingers. Now they would see that he was a friend and he needed help.

He went to the door.

"Hallo!" he called again.

He could hear voices quite distinctly. At last, someone was coming! He heard the sound of huge bolts being shot back, and the door slowly swung open. Oskar looked in horror! It was one of the guards who had seized him and Henrietta and then had run away from the yetis.

The guard put a tray on the table, set a jug of water beside it and grinned at Oskar. "Be good," he said nastily, "or you'll be in trouble."

"But you've got to help me!" cried Oskar. "My friend *is* in trouble. The yetis are going to kill her. They've already killed my mother! See! Look! Look at these bloodstains on her coat. You've got to help me rescue her."

"If the yetis have got your friend, mate, she's done for," said the guard not unsympathetically. "And none of us would try to take on those yetis, I can tell you."

"But you *have* to," insisted Oskar. "*Please!* Take me to your king and let me ask him or whoever it is who runs this palace."

The guard burst out laughing.

"Take you to the Controller," he spluttered. "That's a good one. It'd be the last thing I ever did, I can tell you."

"You don't understand!" cried Oskar. "You've got to let me explain. You must!"

"It's not 'must' anything," snapped the guard. "Now pipe down and eat this and count your lucky stars the yetis haven't got *you.*"

And he went out, bolting the door behind him.

Oskar felt numb. So they weren't kind people who'd rescued him. He'd fallen back into the hands of the guards and this wasn't a palace at all. It was a prison.

He put his head in his hands and stared glumly at the floor.

CHAPTER TWELVE

For a long time, Oskar sat thinking. Could it have been only the day before yesterday that he'd been at home with Elspeth?

"If I ever do get back," vowed Oskar, "I'll never want to go away again."

He should have realised earlier that this room was a cell. It was obvious from the size of the door, the tiny window with its grating, and the lack of furniture. Even the walls were made of blocks of marble set edge to edge. He examined them. They looked solid but perhaps there was a crack or chink somewhere that he could peep through. He ran his fingers over the marble. How strange! It was certainly cool but it wasn't smooth at all: it was very slightly sticky and his fingers made marks on it. Oskar decided to work behind the bed because it would be less noticeable. He dragged it slightly away from the wall, took the spoon from the tray the guard had left and ran the end of the handle down one of the cracks between the blocks.

If he pushed very hard, he could make a slight gap.

What could he use to make it bigger? He scrutinized everything in his cell. Cup, saucer, bowl, plate, bedclothes, table, his own clothing. . . . He took off his right shoe. The floor felt cold through his sock. Using the buckle of his shoe, he ran the sharp point of it up and down the crack. The gap widened. Oskar took the spoon and dug at it again.

Then he did the same thing to the bottom of the block until

he could get his fingers into the space and wiggle the block on two sides. Painstakingly, he started again along the top line and down the other side.

Suddenly he remembered the guard!

"I'd better eat my food now in case he comes back," he thought and he pushed the bed back in place so nothing could be seen, then went over to check what was on the tray. It was an omelette with two slices of wholemeal bread. Oskar started on the omelette. It tasted like egg but it clearly wasn't: just like the soup, there was something odd about it. And the bread was frozen.

"Ice-cold bread! How horrible," thought Oskar but he ate it just the same.

He was about to go back to his efforts with the wallblock when he heard footsteps and the guard reappeared, took the tray with the plates and cutlery, and went away.

"Off to sleep, now," he said to Oskar as he left. "See you in the morning."

Oskar waited till he heard the bolts slide back into position and the footsteps die away before he pulled out the bed again. But the guard had taken away the spoon. He took off his shoe and carried on using the buckle point. It was very slow work and he was beginning to feel it was a waste of time when he heard a faint sound on the other side of the wall. It sounded like somebody tapping. He listened hard. Tap: tap. Tap: tap: tap. Tap: tap. Oskar tapped on the table top with his shoe. There came an answering tap.

"Hallo!" he called softly.

"Hallo!" he heard faintly from behind the wall. The voice said something else but Oskar couldn't catch it. He went to work with renewed fervour on the block, shaking it and tugging it, until finally, slowly, it began to move. Pulling at one side, then the other, he inched it forward out of the surrounding wall and laid it on the floor under the bed.

Trembling with anticipation, he knelt down, put his face to the gap, and peered through. There, in front of him, on the other side of the wall, sat the strangest person he had ever seen in his life!

CHAPTER THIRTEEN

Oskar gasped! The man in the next cell was short, round and pearshaped. He wore a green fur boilersuit with oddlooking badges pinned all over it, a red shawl round his shoulders, heavy black boots, a purple scarf and, on his head, which was quite bald, he had a large conical-shaped brown hat exactly like a huge icecream cone. His face was also round and he had twinkly green eyes, a bulbous nose and a large mouth full of crooked teeth.

Oskar stared at him.

"It's rude to stare," said the little man.

"I'm sorry," said Oskar. "But you look a lot different from the guard."

"So I should hope!" said the little man. "He's a dreadful fellow. Most uncouth."

Oskar didn't know what uncouth was but he felt he ought to agree.

"Yes, he is," he said. "And I didn't think you looked like him at all, really I didn't."

"It's all right," said his cell neighbour. "Don't worry. I'm not offended. What's your name?"

"Oskar."

"And mine," said the little man, "is Ernest Ebenezer Barnsbury Tooks but I'm known as the Great Khone, and that is what you shall call me."

"It's a very long name," said Oskar.

"It is," agreed the Great Khone, "so you may call me Khone for short. Why are you here?"

Oskar related his adventures to the Khone. As he talked about the yetis, the Khone grew very excited.

"Hmm," he kept repeating. And when Oskar had finished he said, "Now, young man, I have two important things to tell you. The first is that it is most unlikely that the yetis had anything to do with your mother's death. I have travelled extensively in these parts and, in my experience, the yetis have never been known to have harmed anyone. It's far more likely that the guards here attacked your mother and her party, and that the yetis found her anorak later and carried it off. They're peaceable animals on the whole and savage, random slaughter is not in their natures, whereas the Controller . . ."

Here he shuddered and ceased talking.

"Who is the Controller?" asked Oskar.

"Ah, the Controller," said the Khone. "A ruthless, vicious creature with a twisted mind. Who knows who the Controller is? Not even the guards know that. But to return to the yetis.

70

Clearly these animals believed your friend was some kind of superior monkey, similar to themselves, but smaller, and they had every intention of making her their queen."

"That's what I thought, too," said Oskar, "and so did Henrietta, but then they took her off."

"I wonder why?" said the Khone. "There must have been a good reason. But I'm certain they have not harmed her."

"I think they have," burst out Oskar, "or else why would they have taken her away?"

"A good question and not easily answered," said the Khone. "Now, young man, slip the block back in position and replace your bed, for in about five minutes the guards will make their evening rounds. After that, we have the whole night to ourselves."

"You told me you had *two* very important things to tell me and you've only really told me one," said Oskar.

"Later," said the Khone. "Quickly! Replace that block and get into bed. The guards will be here shortly so you must be swift, and I promise later I shall tell you. Goodbye for now."

Oskar hastily replaced the block, put his bed back in front of it, climbed under the blankets and closed his eyes. A few minutes later, the door bolts were drawn back and another guard appeared. Oskar feigned sleep. The guard switched off the light and shut and bolted the door.

Oskar waited some time until he was certain the guard had left, then he pulled the bed forward, scrabbled at the block in the dark, removed it and hissed,

"Are you there?"

The Khone's voice came whispering back, "Yes. Now speak quietly. Wrap yourself in your blanket to keep warm and sit close to the gap in the wall. I have a lot to tell you, but first I want to know if you can remove any more blocks. Two more should provide a big enough hole for you to slip through and you can join me in here. The guards won't be back again till morning."

"It's dark," said Oskar. "It'll be hard to see."

"If you wait for about half an hour," said the Khone, "the moon will be up and it's almost full tonight so you'll have a little more light. In the meantime, you and I can have a chat."

"Before we have our chat," said Oskar, "I want to ask you what the walls are made of. It looks like marble and it's cold like marble but it doesn't *feel* like marble. It's sort of sticky. What is it?"

"Marble!" spluttered the Khone and he gave a great guffaw of laughter. "Marble! Oh dear! Oh dear!"

"It's not that funny!" said Oskar, indignantly. "It *does* look like marble."

"Of course it does," agreed the Khone, "But it isn't. Just put your face by the wall, Oskar, and lick it."

"*Lick it?*" cried Oskar. "It might be poisonous."

"It isn't poisonous," said the Khone. "Just lick the wall. You won't come to any harm. Go on, try it."

Oskar put his tongue against the wall and took a lick.

There was a long pause. Then he said incredulously,

"It can't be!"

"It is, though," said the Khone. "What can you taste?"

"If I'm tasting what I think I am," said Oskar, " – and I'm sure I'm not imagining it – these walls aren't made of marble at all. They're made of icecream! Big blocks of icecream!"

CHAPTER FOURTEEN

"Exactly!" said the Khone and he smiled. "Every cell is unique. Every wall and floor is a different flavour. Your cell is strawberry and vanilla and the floor is pineapple."

(Oskar bent down to take a lick at the floor and discovered the Khone was quite right.)

"And the flavours in my cell," went on the Khone, "are quite unlike yours. Far more sophisticated. I used to be in your cell and I know it well, but in this cell I have one wall of grapefruit, one of mango sherbet, one of artichoke, the fourth of parsnip and a floor of tandoori chicken."

"Tandoori chicken ICECREAM!" Oskar was disbelieving.

"It's the Controller, you see," explained the Khone. "Determined to have every known flavour captured in blocks of icecream."

"But why does the Controller want to keep us in prison?" asked Oskar.

"A good question," said the Khone. "In my case there's a special reason, but in your case, I dare say you're wanted as a guinea pig."

"How could I be useful as a guinea pig?"

"To taste the various different icecream flavours," said the Khone.

"That's not so bad," said Oskar. "I love icecream."

"Indeed," said the Khone, "you may love vanilla and chocolate and so on, but you may not be quite so keen on compost, snail with garlic, and castor oil."

"Snail with garlic ICECREAM!" exclaimed Oskar. "That's not possible."

"It is," said the Khone. "I had it just last week and it was horrible."

"It sounds disgusting," said Oskar. "But I still don't understand why the Controller needs someone to do all the taste testing."

"The moon has come up in the last half hour," said the Khone, "and there's more light. Try to make the gap bigger and climb through. I'll push from this side."

Between them, Oskar and the Great Khone managed to loosen and remove three more icecream blocks until there was a hole just large enough for Oskar to squeeze through. Minutes later, he was in the Khone's cell. It was identical to his own. He remarked on this.

"In everything except taste," said the Khone. "Try licking the walls."

"Not the parsnip one," said Oskar. "I hate parsnips and I don't think I'd like tandoori *icecream*."

"Very original," said the Khone. "Highly palatable. I'm rather fond of it myself. They keep moving me around so I've tasted almost all the flavours they've got."

"How many flavours have they got?" Oskar was curious.

"Four thousand and sixty-eight at present," said the Khone, "and I hear they're working on new ones."

"FOUR THOUSAND AND SIXTY-EIGHT ICECREAM FLAVOURS!! That's impossible. There's not that many flavours in the world," exclaimed Oskar.

"Oh, there are, there are," said the Khone.

"But how do you come to be here?" asked Oskar.

"A long story," said the Khone, "and I shall be delighted to tell you all about it later, but there's still the matter of the important thing I have to discuss with you."

"Oh yes," said Oskar. "I completely forgot."

"Quite understandable," said the Khone. "Come and sit down on the bed."

Oskar sat down and pulled the blanket around his shoulders.

"You see," said the Khone, "I've been here rather a long time now. Over a year, in fact. (Oskar shivered. A year seemed an enormously long time to be in prison.) And I've got to know one or two of the guards a little. Some of them are nicer than others and rather more friendly and *they* don't like the Controller either."

"But where do the guards come from?" interrupted Oskar.

"They came with the Controller and it's my belief they were escaped prisoners or in some way in the Controller's power," went on the Khone, "but the point is that one or two of them chat to me. Naturally, the Controller doesn't know about this or they'd be in trouble. Anyway, some of them do talk to me and there's one in particular who was on duty earlier today who told me about you."

"Did he?" Oskar was interested. "What did he say about me?"

"Not much," said the Khone. "Just that they'd brought you in after they'd found you in the snow. I knew you were in the strawberry and vanilla cell, but there is something else I think you ought to know. Get up off my bed and pull it forward like yours."

Oskar did so. Underneath, a block had been removed to create a gap in the wall just like the one Oskar had made.

"You can only do it on the wall where the bed is," said the Khone, "or it would be discovered. And you have to be careful not to damage the blocks on the side that shows. I've had this little peephole for a long time now and it's been very useful."

"If you knew I was in the cell next door, why didn't you shout back to me?" asked Oskar.

"Because I knew the guards were due to come round with food," said the Khone. "And now, I want you to have a look at something."

He drew Oskar down to the gap in the wall.

"There,' he said.

Oskar peered through. The moon had risen even higher in the sky and was shining brightly so that he could see quite clearly. The cell was just like his own. His heart skipped a beat. "I don't believe it," he breathed.

There was someone asleep on the bed, partly covered by a blanket, but, outside the blanket, Oskar could recognise a brown woolly head and two brown gorilla arms.

"It's *Henrietta*!" he cried ecstatically. "She's not dead after all! But how in the world did she get here?"

CHAPTER FIFTEEN

"I don't know," said the Khone, "but she's been here for several hours longer than you. I didn't realise you were together, of course. I thought she was a real gorilla until you told me your story."

"She's asleep," said Oskar regretfully. "I'd really love to talk to her."

"She's had plenty of sleep already today," said the Khone. "Because I thought she was a gorilla, I didn't bother to contact her in case she gave away my peephole." He leaned forward and wiggled another block: it slipped out easily. Then he removed another.

"Climb through there," he offered, "and wake her up, but make sure she doesn't scream or shout."

Oskar wriggled through the gap, went over to the bed, tightly covered Henrietta's mouth with his hand and whispered,

"Henrietta! Wake up! It's me."

Henrietta's eyes opened, then widened in disbelief. "Oskar," she cried, pulling her mouth free. "What are *you* doing here?"

"Ssh," said Oskar, pointing to the hole in the wall with the Khone's face peeping through. "Come in, Khone."

"I can't," sighed the Khone. "I'm too fat. It's all the icecream I eat."

"Don't say 'icecream' to me," said Henrietta. "This whole room's made of it. Every single wall and the floor too."

"So's mine," said Oskar. "The Khone says they all are. Each wall's a different flavour. I've got a pineapple floor, one strawberry and one vanilla wall and . . ."

"Don't tell me," interrupted Henrietta gloomily. "You'll never guess what mine is. It's banana. All banana, every wall and the floor and I expect the ceiling, too, if I could reach it."

Oskar laughed.

"It's because they think you're a monkey and you'll like banana."

"Well, I'm not a monkey and I'm sick of bananas," said Henrietta, "and I'm dying to hear what happened to you."

Oskar suddenly remembered waking up in the empty cave and his anger returned.

"Why did you go off and leave me like that?" he demanded.

"I didn't," said Henrietta. "How could you think I'd do a thing like that?"

"Well, what happened then?"

"Please," interrupted the Khone, "why don't you both come back into my cell so I can hear too?"

They climbed back through the gap into the Khone's cell and sat huddled under the blanket on his bed while Henrietta began her story.

"I was woken in the night by the yeti queen," she said, "and I saw that all the yetis were up and had put away the throne and table."

"I was sort of half awake for a while when they were packing up, but I was so tired I went back to sleep again," said Oskar.

"I didn't hear them at all," went on Henrietta. "The first thing I knew was when the queen woke me and picked me up again and we all started to leave the cave. I couldn't see you

and you didn't answer when I called but I just thought they were bringing you, too.

"It was dark but there was a moon which reflected on the snow so I could see quite well except for when we left the cave. The queen had her baby on her back and me in her arms. She went to the cave entrance and I looked and saw, way above, a tiny chink of moonlit sky. She hesitated just for a moment, then gave a great leap and we soared up to the other side of the precipice. As we left the ground, I looked down and there seemed to be a huge black hole underneath us. I was terrified, because if she'd misjudged we'd have crashed right down into the chasm. But she didn't slip. Clutching with one paw, she pushed me up onto firm ground and over the precipice. Then she hauled herself up. We had just time to roll out of the way before all the other yetis came flying over the edge one after another. I was looking for you everywhere but there were such a lot of them that I gave up. I didn't think for a second they would have left you behind. After all, they took me."

"But they think you're a gorilla," Oskar pointed out.

"I suppose so," said Henrietta. "I keep forgetting that. Maybe I should just take off this gorilla suit now."

'No! No!" said the Khone. "Under no circumstances! The Controller thinks you're a gorilla and it wouldn't do any good to let on you're not. There could be an advantage in being a gorilla."

"As far as I can see," said Henrietta, "the only thing about being a gorilla is that they've given me a banana flavoured cell. Anyway, do you want to hear what happened then?"

"Yes, of course!" said Oskar.

Henrietta resumed her story. "We went on across the snow for quite a long time until, eventually, we came to a sort of mountain and they all went in."

"Went in where?"

"Into the mountain, of course," said Henrietta, irritated. "I wish you'd stop interrupting me."

"But how can you get into a mountain?" asked Oskar.

"There was a tunnel entrance on one side," explained Henrietta. "It wasn't very large. All the yetis had to go in in single file and crouch over, but . . . at the end of the tunnel, suddenly it opened out into a huge room, like a cathedral. I delivered a telegram once to St Paul's Cathedral, and I remember how it looked. And all around were amazing pictures painted straight onto the walls, and real gold statues and some others made of dark blue shiny stone."

"Lapis lazuli, I imagine," remarked the Khone. "Very precious and rare, especially in large pieces."

"And then," continued Henrietta, "the queen took me right up onto a wide platform running round the room above the painted walls, and some more yetis came with another of those white furry skins and they wrapped it round me and put a gold crown on my head. The yetis down in the main part of the cathedral room started shouting and crying out and waving their arms, and then the queen gave a really loud cry and all of them were silent while she chattered away to them in their language. I kept on looking around but I couldn't see you anywhere and I was starting to get worried, when suddenly a great clamour broke out. All the yetis began to run towards the tunnel and in a few minutes they had vanished. The queen and the four yetis left on the platform with me had some kind of conference, then the queen gave me her baby to hold and they disappeared with the crown and the white skin."

"That'll be a snow leopard skin," said the Khone. "They're also rare and hard to come by."

"Gosh," said Henrietta. "I wish I'd known. I'd have been more impressed when I wore it. I just thought it smelt a bit."

"What happened next?" asked Oskar impatiently.

Henrietta looked upset.

"This is the awful part," she said. "I was holding onto the

baby waiting for its mother to come back when, without any warning, two men emerged from the tunnel, and one pointed up to me on the ledge, shouting, "There it is! Capture it!" They threw a huge net up onto the platform and over me and the baby and, as we came tumbling down in it, I hit my head on the edge and I don't remember anything else till I woke up and found I was in the cell. And the worst thing is that I don't know what's happened to the baby."

The Khone looked grave.

"The yeti queen won't like her baby being captured," he said. "She'll be on the warpath and I shouldn't like to be the person who took it when she gets hold of him."

"But how will she know where to look?" asked Oskar.

"Footpaths and scent trails," answered the Khone. "Yetis are highly intelligent beasts."

"Lots of people don't believe yetis exist," said Henrietta.

"They don't want people to know they exist," said the Khone. "They'd only be hunted for museums and zoos and so on, and probably yeti fur coats would be all the fashion. They're too clever to want to join civilisation. But the queen will want her baby back, dead or alive, and she'll hunt for it until she finds it."

"I like the yetis," said Henrietta. "They're cuddly and kind."

"They weren't so kind to me," said Oskar.

"They didn't actually hurt you," said Henrietta, "and maybe they didn't mean to leave you in the cave."

"I imagine that they intended to go back to the cave after the ceremony," said the Khone. "You must remember they are apes and they thought Henrietta was also an ape, so it's natural, Oskar, that they wouldn't want people at their private ape ceremonies. After all, people in general don't usually treat them very well."

"I suppose so," said Oskar.

"And now," said the Khone, "it's time we split up and went to bed."

"I'm so glad we're back together," said Henrietta. "I've been really upset."

"Me too," said Oskar. "I was worried that the yetis had killed you."

"I'll see you tomorrow," said Henrietta.

"At night though," warned the Khone. "The daytime's too dangerous except for a quick whispered word or two."

Oskar and Henrietta clambered back through their gaps and with the Khone's help began replacing blocks till the walls looked normal again. Then all three of them fell fast asleep.

CHAPTER SIXTEEN

Henrietta woke up impatient for it to be night already so she could meet Oskar again in the Khone's cell. Between meals, all of which were banana, she licked the walls to pass the time.

"But I do *hate* banana," she said to herself, "and Oskar and the Khone are having chips and hamburger icecream."

As soon as the guard had made his final rounds, she began to remove the blocks, and climbed through the hole to join Oskar who was already in the Khone's cell. They crawled under the blanket.

"We have to think up a plan to escape," began Henrietta.

"All in good time," said the Khone. "First we must know something more about one another. Oskar told me the sad news about his mother and although we have no idea where his grandmother is at the moment, sooner or later, she will begin making enquiries. Now, what about your parents?" He turned to Henrietta.

Henrietta hung her head. "I haven't got any," she mumbled.

"No *parents*?" cried the Khone. "Impossible. You can't be born if you haven't got parents. What have you done with them?"

"I haven't done anything with them," said Henrietta angrily. "I told you, I just don't have any."

"But who looks after you?" asked the Khone.

"I look after myself," said Henrietta. "I've got a job. I sing telegrams and I'm very good at it. That's why I'm here."

"Oskar told me that," said the Khone. "But where do you live?"

"I've got a room," said Henrietta. "It's quite small but it's nice. It's got yellow walls and a blue door and a bed and a cooker."

"But you shouldn't live on your *own*," said the Khone.

"I have to," explained Henrietta. "I don't have any relations so what else can I do?"

"Aren't you lonely?" asked the Khone.

"No," said Henrietta, much too loudly. "Well, not very often. Sometimes at Christmas and on my birthday, maybe."

"Dear, dear," said the Khone. "What a sorry state of affairs."

"My parents died," said Henrietta. "They were in a car crash about three years ago and I've sort of managed for myself ever since."

Oskar could see that Henrietta was starting to get upset. "What about you, Khone?" he interrupted. "Where do you live?"

The Khone gave a deep sigh. "Ah," he said, "you may well ask. It's a sad story and perhaps you'd rather not hear it."

"I don't mind," said Oskar. "Do you, Henrietta?"

"No," said Henrietta. "Tell us."

The Khone thought for a bit, then he said, "It's a long time since I had anyone to talk to, so I shall begin at the beginning and finish off tomorrow night. Now, here is who I am. As you know, my name is Ernest Ebenezer Barnsbury Tooks. What you may not know is that I am an icecream manufacturer."

"An icecream manufacturer!" cried Henrietta. "So it's *your* palace!"

85

"Ssh!" warned the Khone. "No. No, indeed. It's my icecream (some of it), but not my palace. The palace belongs to the Controller. And no one has ever seen the Controller."

"Why are they afraid of someone they've never seen?" asked Henrietta.

"A good question," said the Khone. "No one sees the Controller, but everyone knows the Controller's wishes. A trusted servant conveys them to the chief guard and he in turn conveys them to the other guards, who do as they are told under threat of punishment. Any guard who disobeys is beaten and thrown into one of the dungeon cells. Any guard who tries to escape is thrown to the snow leopard which the Controller keeps in a pit in the palace vaults, and any guard who criticizes the Controller suffers the most terrible fate of all."

"What's that?" asked Oskar.

"The evil white punishment cell," said the Khone. "It looks dazzlingly clean and beautiful with pure white walls, but each wall is made of a different deadly substance. One wall is made of bleach icecream, another of mothball mixture, another of rat poison and the fourth of plaster-of-paris which cements up your insides. Prisoners in the deadly white cell are never given food or water, so in desperation they lick the walls and, whichever one they choose, they die in agony."

"How awful," said Oskar. "What are the dungeon cells made of?"

"Slime, mould and woodlice flavour," said the Khone.

"Yuk!" said Henrietta. "Woodlice flavour!"

"So the walls are coloured green and greyish black. Very depressing," continued the Khone.

"But how do you know?" asked Henrietta.

"Because I was in one for a time," said the Khone, "and a horrible time it was, too. I refused to divulge my secrets to the Controller, so I was put into a dungeon cell."

"And did you tell in the end?" Oskar was curious.

"There was no need to," answered the Khone. "The Controller found out without my help, so I was moved back up here again."

"But how did you get here at all if you were an icecream manufacturer? And who buys *icecream* in the Himalayas?" Henrietta asked.

"Ah," said the Khone, "I wasn't in the Himalayas making icecream, I was in England. I had a dreadful experience when I was a child and as a result, later on, I decided to buy a factory and make icecream. And what icecream that was!" Here he sighed dreamily and broke off. "Fig, cherry, gooseberry, raspberry and melon. 'Tooks' Toffee Twirly Twists,' 'Ebenezer's Easter-Egg Ecstasies' . . ."

"What were they?" asked Henrietta.

"Ummm," said the Khone. "A dark chocolate outer layer with a luscious raspberry icecream inner layer and a tiny chick made of pineapple marshmallow inside. Then there were 'Ernest's Exciting Exotic Fruit Fantasies', 'Barnsbury's Blueberry-Blackberry Bombes' and many, many more. I was very happy and contented. Every year I supplied all the orphanages in the country with icecream for Christmas and Easter. My icecream was shipped to far-off foreign countries, and I employed a whole laboratory of chemists to help me search out newer and better flavours. What a happy man I was!" He sighed. "It was about this time that people began to call me The Great Khone and I took to wearing icecream cone hats. Then, one day, came a terrible disaster.

"A shop returned my icecreams. 'They're not good enough. Something tastes wrong,' the shop manager explained. I had them brought straight up to my office and tasted them myself. Something was indeed very wrong. Every block tasted slightly bitter and burnt my tongue when I licked it. I was horrified. I rushed to the laboratories and had the chemists analyse the samples immediately.

"An hour later, the results were sent up. The icecream had been doctored with bitter aloes! But who could have done such a shocking thing? I racked my brains but could think of no one. Next morning, when I arrived early in my office to ponder over the problem, there was a letter waiting for me. I tore it open. It said simply, 'SELL ME YOUR STOCKS OR I WILL RUIN YOU.'

"The top detectives in the country could not trace the sender, but the postmark was the Himalayas so, by that afternoon, I was on my way there in a plane. As soon as I arrived I was handed a telegram. 'RETURN IMMEDIATELY,' it said. 'DESPERATE SITUATION. URGENT.' And it was signed by my chief chemist.

"I flew back at once and raced in a taxi to the factory. The chief chemist was waiting for me and led me to the refrigerated storerooms. He flung open the double doors and a blast of icy air wafted out. I looked in. Where were the icecreams? All the freezers were empty. 'Stolen,' said the chief chemist, brokenly. 'Every cone, block, gateau and bombe. All gone, overnight.'

"And in every icecream factory all over the country, the same thing had taken place. There was not a spoonful of icecream to be had anywhere in England."

"I remember," broke in Oskar. "My grandmother tried to

buy it but our grocer's shop said they couldn't get any."

'Why didn't we see it on television or read about it in the papers?" asked Henrietta.

"Scotland Yard decided to keep it quiet," said the Khone, "because they couldn't trace the criminals. And things got worse. Without the money from the sales of the stolen icecream no one could afford to make any more. Icecream had disappeared from the face of Britain! Then we discovered that all over the world the situation was the same. Someone had stolen the world's icecream!"

CHAPTER SEVENTEEN

"No wonder I couldn't buy any!" exclaimed Henrietta.

"But why did the Controller *want* to steal all the icecream in the world?" asked Oskar.

"It's part of a wicked plan," said the Khone. "The Controller, whoever he is, is a most evil person. He wanted to build a palace from icecream bricks with bombes and cones for decoration on the turrets. Of course, then he had to choose a very cold climate to stop the bricks from melting, so he obviously decided upon the Himalayas. Not many people come to this remote region, and it was one of the few places where such a palace could be built without attracting attention. When I first arrived," he recalled mournfully, "I recognised my own Magic Miracle Monster Multi-Licks up on the belltower as gargoyles."

"What are Magic Miracle Monster Multi-Licks?" asked Oskar and Henrietta.

"They're wonderful icecreams on crooked sticks," said the Khone. "Each one has a hideous monster face and as you lick it the face changes to an even worse one until, right at the end, it changes to a vampire tooth that prickles your tongue like sherbet and spurts out strawberry icecream as you crunch it."

"I'd really like one!" cried Henrietta.

"Well, you'd have to climb up to the belfry tower to get one now," said the Khone. "And, as well, there's my Crunchy Crackly Popcorn Iceballs, full of nutrition and ideal for the family breakfast, all the goodness of cereal in a nutty, chewy icecream. *They've* been used to decorate the outside of all the palace windows. And I saw my Gooseberry and Raspberry Striped Icecream, my British Blackberry Blocks and many, many others built into the palace walls.

"I came here, you see, to do a little investigation of my own. Scotland Yard wasn't getting any closer to a solution and as I went to bed one night I thought, 'Why would anyone need that much icecream? It's enough to build a city with.' Then, suddenly, I realised that that was it! And I got out of bed, took the atlas and looked at the really cold spots of the world. Antarctica seemed too far away. That left only the Himalayas or the mountains of South America or the Arctic Circle, and somehow I felt the Himalayas was the place. After all, the postmark on my message had come from there.

"So I set out the next day and when I got here, I travelled

until I heard rumours about a huge palace over the mountain chain and I finally discovered it. That was when I met the yetis and found them kind and intelligent."

"And how were you captured?" asked Oskar.

"Through my own stupidity," answered the Khone. "I believed that if only I could meet the Controller, I could persuade him that what he was doing was terribly wrong. I was prepared to offer him shares in my own icecream business in return for his agreeing to return the icecream. But the guards seized me and flung me into the dungeons. Upon discovering who I was, the Controller sent a messenger to try to enlist my services to help him. Not only does he wish to control all the icecream in the world, but he has an evil plan to control the world itself.

"For months, a team of chemists has been experimenting with new icecream flavours that no one has ever considered before – soap, turnip, pickle and so on. There's even a mixed Chinese-takeaway icecream with icecream beansprouts. And, the guard tells me, (though he shouldn't), that in some way the Controller intends to take over the world using icecream. The guard doesn't know the details but he's heard about the general plan. And when the takeover is complete, the Controller will rule the world."

"That's appalling," said Henrietta. "Surely there must be some way to stop him."

"Very few people even know of his existence," pointed out the Khone. "And the guard told me only yesterday that there is great excitement in the laboratories because an amazing new discovery has occurred. I'm afraid this may be what the Controller has been waiting for."

"There's only one thing you haven't told us," said Oskar. "What was the dreadful thing that happened when you were young that made you decide to be an icecream manufacturer?"

The Khone thought for a bit. "I think I *will* tell you," he said finally. "Usually I don't ever talk about it, but as we are friends here in adversity, I shall relate my story to you. Now, off you go so we can put back the blocks, and tomorrow, I promise, you shall hear it."

The next night, Oskar and Henrietta clambered into the Khone's cell as soon as the guard had left for the night.

"Banana icecream *again*!" said Henrietta. "You'd think they'd give me peanut or something. It's even worse because I know you two are having roast beef icecream. I can't stand it much longer. We'll have to try to escape."

"Escape!" cried the Khone, alarmed. "Why do we need to escape?"

"Of *course* we want to escape!" said Henrietta. "You must have thought of ways to get out. You've been here more than a year."

Oskar felt it was a mistake for Henrietta to start talking about escaping so soon. He decided to change the subject.

"Why don't you tell us about the terrible thing that happened to you when you were a boy?" he said.

"Do you really want to hear?" asked the Khone.

"Of course we do," said Oskar, throwing Henrietta a warning look.

"Well," said the Khone, rather pleased, "if you *want* to hear that's different. Now, are you sitting comfortably?"

Henrietta scowled.

"How could anyone be comfortable in prison?" she muttered. The Khone ignored this.

"As I told you, it's a long story," he said, "so I shall start at once."

CHAPTER EIGHTEEN

"When I was a small boy," began the Khone, "I had a kind, loving nanny called Nanny Granderby. She and I went for walks in the park, made toast in front of the fire, cut out paper dolls, and went to the seaside in Summer. Every Sunday, we went to the Science Museum and afterwards we bought a big icecream cone. One Sunday it would be vanilla, the next chocolate, the next strawberry and the next raspberry ripple. And all week I looked forward to my Sunday icecream with Nanny Granderby.

"Then one morning Nanny Granderby was gone and the same evening my new governess arrived. I heard a car drive up to the house and peered from the nursery window. Out stepped a figure dressed from head to foot in dismal black. I couldn't see properly because it was getting dark, but a shudder ran down my spine as I watched.

"The butler took her trunks and she picked up something from inside the cab, but what it was I couldn't make out through the evening mist. Then, after about half an hour, my great-aunt brought her up to the nursery. 'Ernest,' she said, 'this is your new governess, Miss Cripplegate.'

"Miss Cripplegate stepped forward. She was tall and thin. The skin of her face was deathly white and stretched tightly over her cheekbones so that her face looked almost like a skull. Her hair was black and drawn back into a tight bun, and she wore a long black skirt, a black blouse with jet beads and black

shoes and stockings. The only things about her that were not black were her chalk white skin and her eyes, which were a pale greenish yellow and looked exactly like marbles. 'Hello, little boy,' she said and reached out to take my hand. Her touch was light and clammy. 'And this,' she said, 'is my dear friend and companion, Balthazzar. Come out, Balthazzar, and meet our new pupil.' She shook her wide sleeve and out popped a sleek white ferret!

"My great-aunt screamed and leapt back. 'Please!' cried Miss Cripplegate. 'Balthazzar is very delicate. Don't scream like that or you'll upset him.'

"The ferret curled its lip and showed its pointed teeth. Miss

Cripplegate reached down and stroked it, then she stowed the horrible thing back in her sleeve again. 'And now,' she said, 'we begin lessons immediately.'

"'Really, Miss Cripplegate,' protested my great-aunt, 'it's very late and nearly bedtime. Lessons need not start till the day after tomorrow. Tomorrow can be a holiday.'

"'Tomorrow, we shall begin lessons at eight o'clock SHARP!' said Miss Cripplegate. 'No time like the present. Time flies, and an hour spent in idle pleasure is an hour wasted. Now Balthazzar and I must unpack. I shall sleep in the nursery with my new little boy. I feel sure we shall grow to understand each other VERY soon.'

"'As you wish, Miss Cripplegate,' said my great-aunt. 'Dinner will be served downstairs at nine o'clock sharp.'

"'Thank you, but no dinner for me,' said Miss Cripplegate. 'I never leave the schoolroom and the nursery except on nursery business.'

"'Perhaps we can discuss it tomorrow,' said my great-aunt.

"'*After* lessons,' said Miss Cripplegate.

"Great-aunt went out and I was left alone with Miss Cripplegate and her ferret.

"'So, little boy,' hissed Miss Cripplegate, 'what a miserable, snivelling brat you are, to be sure. Stand under the light so I can see you properly.'

"I went and stood by the central nursery light.

"'Ugly creature, isn't he, Balthazzar?' remarked Miss Cripplegate. 'A disgusting young boy who will have to learn to BEHAVE HIMSELF.' And, leaning very close to my face, she snarled, 'I *hate* small boys: I loathe and despise them. Nasty repulsive little beasts. Tell me, you horrible young fellow, how old are you?'

" 'Seven,' I stammered.

" 'Seven,' said Miss Cripplegate. 'I see. Seven. *So*, we will study seven hours a day in the nursery tomorrow and you will have *seven* minutes for lunch and a *seven* minute walk in the afternoon, and Balthazzar,' (here her tone changed to loving tenderness), 'my darling Balthazzar, will have seven special chocolates after his supper tonight. Now get to bed!'

"I cried myself to sleep remembering kind Nanny Granderby.

"Miss Cripplegate was as good as her word. Every day she sat me down with my books for seven hours, and when I got my schoolwork wrong, she boxed my ears or, even worse, ordered Balthazzar to climb out of her sleeve and nip my shins. Then it was Sunday.

" 'Because it is Sunday and a holy day of rest,' announced Miss Cripplegate, 'you will not do schoolwork, but you will pray on your knees for two hours to improve your wickedness.'

" 'But Miss Cripplegate,' I said, 'on Sundays, Nanny Granderby and I went to the Science Museum and afterwards we had an icecream cone.'

" 'Balthazzar does not like the Science Museum,' said Miss Cripplegate, 'so you will not be going there again. Instead, we will take a health-giving walk in the cemetery and afterwards I will instruct Cook to have icecream sent up to the nursery.'

"No more Science Museum! No more icecream cones! No more toasting muffins by the nursery fire with dear Nanny Granderby.

" 'Miss Cripplegate!' I cried in despair.

" 'Be quiet, beastly boy!' she said.

"Sunday came. By lunchtime I was stiff and sore from kneeling at prayers and it was only the thought of icecream for supper that kept me from crying.

"After lunch, Miss Cripplegate put on her black coat and hat and we set off for the cemetery. It had been raining and the tombstones looked dank and dripping, the ground was squelchy and I longed to get away and be back in the warm nursery. But Balthazzar liked this dismal place. He slithered amongst the gravestones and sniffed the misty air with delight.

"'Dear Balthazzar loves graveyards,' remarked Miss Cripplegate. 'Last time we visited one he found a dead owl.' And she stroked the ferret. My feet ached with cold and I stood shivering by the marble headstones as Balthazzar ran back and forth among the graves.

"Finally Miss Cripplegate decided it was time to go home.

"'At least there will be icecream for supper,' I thought to myself as I trudged along.

"'Hurry up!' snapped Miss Cripplegate.

"'My feet are too cold,' I said.

"'Weakling!' she cried.

"At last we were in the nursery in front of the blazing fire. Up came the supper tray and there in the middle of it was an enormous dish of strawberry icecream! My spirits rose. I was reaching out for it when suddenly, Miss Cripplegate leaned forward and snatched it away. 'Icecream,' she said, 'is a poison to growing children! You shall never again swallow a mouthful while you are in my charge!' And she put the dish down on the floor.

"'Balthazzar,' she called. 'Here, my treasure. Supper treats for pretty ferrets.'

"The ferret raced out of her sleeve and onto the dish and gobbled up my precious icecream. A tear slid down my cheek. 'Crybaby,' said Miss Cripplegate. 'Go to bed.'

"And so for the next few years, every Sunday, the cook sent up a large dish of delicious homemade icecream and every Sunday, Balthazzar ate it. How I hated him.

"Sometimes, at night, Miss Cripplegate would sit him on my pillow where he would snap his sharp pointed teeth at me and gaze at me nastily. Sometimes he would nip my ankle and draw blood. And sometimes, he would race up my leg, across my body and down my arms, like some evil white rat, breathing and squeaking as he ran.

"Then, one day, Miss Cripplegate and Balthazzar were gone. I woke up and they weren't there. The nursery was empty. I called and called and then realised, with a tremendous surge of relief, that the black carpet bag was gone too, and they had left for ever. I was overjoyed.

"But occasionally," (here the Great Khone gave a shiver) "just occasionally, I still wake from a nightmare where Miss Cripplegate has come back and Balthazzar is creeping over me again."

Oskar and Henrietta had sat quietly throughout the story.

"So that's why you don't mind being in prison," said Oskar.

"I do mind," said the Khone, "but it's made a lot better by the fact that you can eat as much icecream as you want here."

"All I've had is banana flavour," complained Henrietta, "except for the occasional licks of the Khone's walls."

"Don't start that again," said Oskar. "I'm sorry for you but we can't do anything about it and at least it's better than that awful food we had with the yetis. Anyway, my icecream's not always nice. I had pepper flavour yesterday."

"The Controller must be experimenting," said the Khone. "I wonder why."

"Well, I'm completely sick of icecream," said Oskar. "I've had enough to last me forever."

"I think it's time you were getting back to your cells," said the Khone.

"I liked hearing your story," said Henrietta. "Miss Cripplegate sounded really creepy. No wonder you hated her."

"A terrible creature," said the Khone. "Never mind. She's long since gone. Now, off you go quickly and I'll see you tomorrow night. Sleep well!"

CHAPTER NINETEEN

Back in bed in her own cell, Henrietta felt uneasy and couldn't sleep.

"I like the Khone," she thought, "and he's kind, but he's been in prison for *months* and he doesn't seem to want to get out."

She recalled the dreamy look on the Khone's face whenever he talked about icecream.

"He doesn't want to leave," she thought. "He wants to be where his icecream is. I've got to get to Oskar and talk to him by myself."

But how could she? The Khone's cell was in between.

"I'll wait till he's asleep," she decided.

Some time later she heard through the gap the sound of heavy snoring coming from the Khone's cell. Gently, she removed the blocks and slid through under his bed. She wriggled out silently, slipped across to the other wall, carefully pushed out the blocks, and crawled through the hole in the wall.

"Oskar," she whispered.

Oskar, who had only just closed his eyes and was barely asleep, woke up immediately.

"Ssh!" continued Henrietta. "We've got to get out of here. We have to work out a plan. I like the Khone but he doesn't *do* anything. We ought to be trying to get away, not just sitting round talking."

Oskar sat up. "I know," he agreed, "but what can we do?"

"Let's think about it and meet again," said Henrietta. "We can pool our ideas."

They talked for a little while longer, then Henrietta went back to her own cell where she fell into a deep sleep.

She was awoken by the noise of the bolt being drawn back. There stood the guard with her breakfast. Banana icecream! Henrietta pulled an ugly gorilla face. She was good at this from her telegram practice.

The guard drew back in alarm. "All right, all right," he said. "No need to get nasty then."

"He's scared of gorillas," thought Henrietta, and she moved towards him snarling a bit. The guard backed out quickly leaving the tray behind. Suddenly, Henrietta had a wonderful idea.

At lunchtime when the guard came back with another tray of food, she was lying on her bed, motionless.

"Wake up!" called the guard. Henrietta didn't stir.

"Get up, you ugly monkey," said the guard.

Again Henrietta didn't move. The guard put down the tray and came across to peer at her. He leaned over.

"Is something wrong with you?" he asked.

Quick as a flash, Henrietta leapt to her feet, snarling and growling, and waving her arms menacingly at him. The guard backed away. Henrietta bared her teeth in a ferocious grimace and snapped nastily. He edged to the door. She followed him. Suddenly, as he was almost through, she leapt at him, attacking him with her fists.

"Help!" screamed the guard, and raced off down the corridor. Henrietta ran to the Khone's door and unbolted it. "Quick!" she panted. "Hurry! You're free!"

"Henrietta!" cried the Khone. "What on earth are you doing here?"

"Hurry UP!" shouted Henrietta. "I've freed you. Come OUT!"

She tugged at the bolt on Oskar's door, wrenched it back and flung the door open. He ran out to join her.

"How marvellous! You're so clever!" he cried, in jubilation.

The Khone was looking worried. He kept glancing round and almost seemed ready to go back into his cell.

"What's wrong?" asked Oskar. "Aren't you pleased to be free?"

"I fear," said the Khone, "that we won't be free for very long. You seriously underestimate the power of the Controller. Perhaps we should just go back in and pretend the guard provoked Henrietta."

"*Provoked* her?" Oskar was amazed. "Go back *in*? Why?"

"I'm afraid of the Controller's reprisals," said the Khone.

Henrietta was getting impatient. "Look," she said, "I didn't let you out so we could all stand round and have a conference. Let's hurry up and get out of here. Any minute now that guard will give the alarm. Follow me!"

And she set off along the sloping corridor and up a staircase leading into a large hallway. Here she paused and the other two stopped behind her and watched as she peered cautiously around, then, deciding the coast was clear, led them across the wide expanse of the hall and over to another smaller passage.

"Listen!" said the Khone.

They stopped again and strained to hear. Far away they could hear clamouring and shouting.

"It's the guards!" whispered the Khone. "What shall we do?"

"Quick," said Henrietta. "Into that room over there."

They slithered down the passage into a large green room ("Mint, I expect," remarked the Khone) and hid behind the sofa. The shouting grew louder, then they heard heavy footsteps and the guards came pounding through the hallway they had just crossed. Henrietta's heart was thumping with fright, Oskar's hands shook, and beads of sweat broke out on the Khone's forehead.

"Oh dear!" he kept sighing.

"SSSHH!" hissed Henrietta. "Don't make a sound."

The footsteps and the noises died away again, and the three of them crept out from behind the sofa, back into the passage.

"Look ahead," cried Oskar, excitedly. "Look! Look! It's the main entrance." He slipped in front and peeped round the corner.

The entrance was empty. All the guards must have gone to join in the chase. Any minute now they would return in pursuit when they discovered there was no trace of the three of them downstairs. He beckoned to the Khone and Henrietta, went up to the vast doors and turned the brass handle. It opened. As they went out into the sunlight, the whiteness of the snow dazzled them. The Khone turned back and began to lick the doorhandle.

"What are you DOING?" whispered Henrietta.

"Unbelievable," said the Khone. "Quite outstanding. I thought to myself it must be pineapple or perhaps even burnt butterscotch, but would you believe it's genuine brass? Brass-flavoured icecream. The Controller's diabolical, of course, but clever, fiendishly clever. Imagine that, *brass* icecream."

Oskar and Henrietta looked at each other.

"Khone," said Henrietta, "it's terribly important that you try to forget about icecream and hurry up. We've got no time to lose. Please. We're trying to get away before they catch us."

"I'm too fat," said the Khone tearfully. "I'll never make it. You go on without me."

"We can't do that," said Oskar. "Now, TRY. Don't be so hopeless. We'll help you." He felt really exasperated. Didn't the Khone realise the danger they were in?

"If we can just make it to that ridge over there, we can dig ourselves a hole in the snow and hide there till the danger's over," he promised. "Come on."

They all floundered across the snow and, with Henrietta pushing and Oskar pulling, they managed somehow to drag the Khone along with them. Over the ridge they staggered, and scrabbled and dug until they had a reasonable sized hole in the ground, then they all squeezed in together and waited.

Not a sound floated to them. They were very squashed and

cold in the hole. Oskar's face was hot from the sun and his bottom was frozen and damp from the snow. He cocked his head and listened but there was no noise at all. He waited for quite a long time, then he leaned across to Henrietta and whispered, "I think we've given them the slip. Shall we climb out now?"

She shook her head. "Not just yet."

Oskar adjusted his position a little, leaned back and looked up. He screamed!

There, behind him, in a semi-circle stood the guards, watching them.

"Clever, aren't you?" said the chief guard. "But not clever enough. You left a very clear path for us to follow – three trails of footprints in the snow!"

CHAPTER TWENTY

Oskar sat dejectedly in the cell he was now sharing with Henrietta and the Khone. He had a long chain round his left ankle, attached to a ring set into the wall.

"And it won't pull out, if that's what you think," the guard had assured him. "Only half this wall's icecream. The rest is the solid rock that the whole castle's built on. I wouldn't like to be in your shoes, mate, when the Controller gets to hear about your escape. And keep that flaming monkey under control."

For Henrietta had managed to bite the guards several times as they'd been dragged back into the palace. "Savage brute. It ought to be destroyed," went on the guard.

Henrietta snarled at him. It was a different guard from the one they'd had before.

"Pipe down," he said nastily, and vanished.

They heard the sound of a key turning in the lock and the grating of the bolts being shot across the door.

"Footprints," said Oskar bitterly. "Why didn't we think of them?"

The Khone was sitting sadly on an upturned box, the only furniture in the cell.

"Castor oil icecream," he muttered. "A dreadful, disgusting taste. I shall never get rid of it."

Henrietta, on the other hand, was restless. She kept walking round and round the box and kicking at it.

"When I get home," she promised, "I'll make the Post Office sorry for this. It's all wrong." And she kicked the box again savagely.

"Do STOP IT, you two!" said Oskar. "At least let's not be gloomier than we have to be. It doesn't help."

"We aren't going to be kept here for long," said the Khone. "There aren't any beds."

"Well, as long as we are here," said Oskar, "why don't you tell us more about your icecream flavours?"

The Khone brightened. "But do you really want to hear?" he said. "Won't it just make us all feel worse?"

"I couldn't feel worse," said Henrietta. "You might as well tell us."

"All right," said the Khone, "but what do you want to hear about?"

"Did you make icecream sundaes?" asked Oskar. "I like those."

"Sundaes!" cried the Khone. "Of course! And not just Sundaes, but Mondaes, Tuesdaes, Wednesdaes, Thursdaes, Fridaes and Saturdaes. And such original flavour combinations! Chocolate and tomato, peanut and bacon, ketchup and prune, sardine and vanilla, fish and chip and porridge, and black pudding and strawberry. Then, on November the Fifth, we always had Flying Firework Fizzers. You put your tongue through the hole in the centre of the Fizzer, spit on the touchpaper, and it starts to spin round and round. And, as it spins, it shoots off different icecream flavours into your mouth."

"Yum!" said Oskar.

"Then," went on the Khone, "there were Hallowe'en Horrors: gruesome masks you wear to terrorize your friends and

family and later, as you lick them, they turn into glowing Jack-o'-Lanterns with either a trick or treat flavour – strawberry, vanilla and chocolate for treats, and flour, spinach or drainwater for tricks.

"And then there were Whizzbezookers that make loud rude noises as you suck them, Lucky Licks . . ."

"What's a Lucky Lick?"

"A surprise icecream dip," said the Khone. "It starts off tasting of bran, just like a brantub, then there's a layer of wrapping-paper flavour, then a surprise treat or small present on your tongue. And Raspberry Rhubarb Raisin' Rolls that make your heels rise off the ground as you eat, and Icecream Tricks, when your tongue sticks to the icecream.

"But, best of all, were my Almond Autos and Bilberry Build-a-Bikes! Make your own vehicle from parts concealed in our delicious icecreams. Buy twenty thousand icecreams and you can assemble your own car, or with only twelve thousand, you can build a bicycle, and we will supply a *free* ignition key or bicycle lock!"

"Look!" shrieked Henrietta suddenly. "Over there! Quick!"

The Khone broke off and looked around.

"Where?" asked Oskar, puzzled. "I can't see anything."

Henrietta shivered. "Something disgusting and white just flashed across the room. It was only little but it was horrible. It's gone now."

"Are you sure you didn't imagine it?" said the Khone. "It's awfully spooky in here."

"No, I didn't," insisted Henrietta. "I *definitely* saw something. It was sort of slippery and white, and really malevolent."

"Well, it's not here now, anyhow," said Oskar, "so why don't you go on telling us about your icecream, Khone?'

"There were some more I wanted to describe to you," began the Khone. "You see, we had a special laboratory for flavour inventing, so . . ." He broke off at the sound of a noise in the corridor. They looked at one another.

"It's not mealtime," said the Khone nervously. "I think it's someone coming to tell us what's going to happen to us."

The cell door opened.

CHAPTER TWENTY-ONE

One of the guards came in. "Come on, you," he said to Henrietta. "You and your friends are wanted upstairs. Special occasion. The Controller's going to be present in person. Big event, I can tell you. Hurry up, now." And he pushed her roughly.

"Don't do that!" cried Oskar. "Leave her alone."

"Shut up, brat," snarled the guard, and he unlocked their chains and propelled them into the corridor.

"Come on, you ugly monkey," he said to Henrietta. "You're needed too."

"You're pretty ugly, yourself," said Henrietta.

The guard swung round. "Who said that?" he asked sharply.

"It was me," said Oskar. "Where are we going?"

"None of your business," said the guard. "Ask no questions and you'll be told no lies. Come along, Grandpa," he added to the Khone, who was lagging behind.

"If I *were* your grandfather," said the Khone, "which, incidentally, I'm very glad I'm not, your manners would be considerably better than they are."

"Oh, listen to him," said the guard. "Now, forward march and follow me. And no tricks!" He set off down the corridor.

"What did you do that for?" whispered Oskar to Henrietta. "You promised you wouldn't talk when anyone else was around. If the guards hear you they'll know you're not a real gorilla."

Henrietta blushed under her woolly suit. "Sorry," she mumbled.

As they went along, the Khone took an occasional lick at the walls. "Mm," he whispered to Henrietta and Oskar from time to time. "Delicious! That one's orange sherbert," or "Amazing! Liquorice!" or "I can't be sure, but that one is quite revolting, and I *think* it's washing-up liquid flavour. Really!!"

As they walked along, Oskar noticed they seemed to be winding upwards. Then, suddenly, the corridor opened out into a broad hallway.

The Khone took another large lick at one of the walls.

"Aah! It can't be!" he breathed, and took a bigger lick.

"Stop that AT ONCE!' commanded the guard. "You're making tongue marks on the wall. The Controller will be furious and I'll be in trouble."

"Freezia flavour," murmured the Khone dreamily. "And that pale purple splash is lavender, and the darker one's violet. Utterly amazing. I realise the Controller's *terrible*, of course, but what a genius of invention. Flower flavoured icecreams."

"*Will* you shut up?" said the guard. "You're barmy, you are. You never get sick of the stuff, do you?"

"It's my passion," confessed the Khone. "I live for icecream."

"Well, you won't have much longer to live for it by the looks of things," said the guard nastily. "Live for it and die for it, by what I hear."

Oskar and Henrietta exchanged anxious looks.

"Whatever do you mean?" asked Oskar.

"For goodness' sake," said the guard. "Don't be daft. You don't think the Controller's brought you here for a party, do you?"

"We don't know why we've been brought here," said Oskar, "but we'd certainly like to. What did you mean 'live for it and die for it'?"

"Look," muttered the guard, "I'm only a guard. Right. Got it. I don't know nothing. None of their decisions got anything to do with me."

"But you heard something?" said Oskar.

" 'Course," said the guard. "Look, I don't know why I'm bothering with telling you anyhow, specially after all the trouble I've had from that blooming monkey."

And he scowled at Henrietta.

"Go on, please," begged Oskar.

"All right then," said the guard, "but you won't like it much I can tell you. I've heard, only *heard*, mind you, that the Controller's got a plan. Planning to test out a new product, you might say."

"No more icecream, you mean?" interrupted the Khone.

"Ssh!" said Oskar. "Don't stop him now."

"Well," continued the guard, "the rumour is the Controller's got some plan for something new and they need subjects for testing it on, and you lot was selected."

"Why us?" asked Oskar.

"You ran away and caused all that trouble," explained the guard. "The Controller didn't like that I can tell you. That's never happened before. No one's never run away like that and it was only a lucky chance you was picked up at all."

"Unlucky for us," said Oskar.

The guard ignored this. "So when volunteers was needed for this new project, naturally you lot was the first to be selected."

"But that's not being a volunteer," objected Oskar. "Being a volunteer means you offer to do something."

"Not here it doesn't mean that," said the guard with a laugh. "Volunteering's a lot different to that here. Here a volunteer's someone the Controller chooses. And you lot's the volunteers right now."

"But what are we volunteering *for*?" asked Oskar.

"A special mission, so I believe," said the guard. "Something to do with a dream the Controller's had for years. Very far-sighted the Controller is. Not content with small ambitions: not wanting little triumphs and victories like the rest of us. No. Not a bit of it. Our Controller wants to control the world. And what you're volunteering to test is going to help to make that happen."

"If your Controller wants to control the world, then your Controller's mad," said Oskar. "That's crazy."

The guard cuffed his ear hard. "You mind your language!" he cried. "Our Controller will succeed. This palace will be the centre of the world when the formula has been perfected. And you lot are going to be the testers. For months the Controller's had the laboratories working at a secret formula and now it's ready. And today we're all going to see the final result and *you* are going to be the ones what show us that result. So just mind your manners – especially you," – and he turned to Henrietta and glowered at her, "because, today, very soon, right here in this room we're coming to, you're going to meet the Controller, face to face."

"How wonderful," enthused the Khone. "When I meet the Controller, I must enquire exactly how those perfect flower flavours were developed."

Oskar looked desperately at Henrietta. "I don't think he realises," he whispered.

"Leave him. You can't do anything about it," Henrietta whispered back. "Are you scared?"

"No," said Oskar stoutly. "Not at all. Well, yes, actually, I am. Look, my hands are shaking."

"I'm scared, too," admitted Henrietta. "I don't feel like dying yet and my leg hurts from the chain."

"Ssh!" said Oskar. "We're there."

The guard flung the huge door open and stepped to one side. Oskar, Henrietta and the Khone stood on the threshold and peered in.

CHAPTER TWENTY-TWO

The entire room was black! The walls were black, the ceiling was black and the carpet was black. About fifty black-clothed guards stood around the room and at a large black table sat seven people with bunsen burners and test-tubes in front of them.

"Chemists," whispered the Khone to Oskar.

"Bring them in!" called one of the chemists and the guard pushed them into the room ahead of him.

"How very bizarre," said the Khone. "I wonder what flavour that wall is. Ah, liquorice, I expect."

"No, blackberry," said Oskar. "See, it's got blackberries squashed in it."

"Those," said one of the chemists haughtily, "are *not* blackberries, they are dead flies. Dead flies in flyspray flavoured icecream, as a matter of fact."

Oskar pulled a face.

"You may sneer," said the chemist, "but this room is totally free of flies, fleas, wasps, spiders, rats, mice and two-tooth borer. It's probably the only room in the world without carpet beetles, house mite and woodworm."

Oskar privately thought that it was very unlikely that any of those could exist for long in such a cold climate anyway, but decided to say nothing.

"Stand up straight!" ordered another of the chemists. 'You

have been brought here before the Council of Chemists to hear the sentence passed upon you for escaping from the palace."

"Why shouldn't we try to escape from prison?" said Oskar.

"Shut up!!" thundered the chemist. "I am the Chief Chemist and I say you are all guilty."

"But we haven't had a trial," objected Oskar.

"There are no trials here," said the Chief Chemist. He picked up a small black skullcap from the table and put it on.

"And your punishment," he continued, "is *death*."

"Death to the traitors!" everyone shouted. The Khone looked in dismay at Oskar and Henrietta.

"I tried to warn you," he said, "but you didn't believe me."

"No talking at all!" shouted the Chief Chemist. "However,

you are very fortunate in your deaths, because the Controller . . ." here all the chemists and guards momentarily bowed their heads . . . "yes, the Controller alone will decide the manner of your execution. Be seated and wait for the Controller's arrival."

As there was nowhere else to sit, Oskar, Henrietta and the Khone sat down on the rug. They had been seated for a few minutes when there was a stir amongst the others and suddenly everyone stood up to attention.

"Get up," said their guard. "Don't you have no manners? Show a bit of respect."

The three of them struggled to their feet. Oskar craned his neck to see over the crowd. Their guard prodded him in the ribcage. "Be quiet," he hissed, "and keep that monkey under control."

Oskar stood on tiptoe to catch his first glimpse of the dreaded Controller. He felt the way he did before he went to the dentist. The guard in front of him moved slightly and the Controller came into view wearing a long black robe with a black hood and black gloves. He carried a large black tray with a cover over it. Oskar shuddered. The Controller certainly *felt* evil.

The black robed figure glided slowly towards the table and Oskar noticed a place set at the end and a large elaborately carved ebony chair in front of it. That must be the Controller's! What frightful thing was he going to do to them? Why, oh why, hadn't Elspeth arrived home and missed him and started a search for him? Would they be executed straight away or would they have to go back to prison? "And I don't even know what's happened to the ice-pick!" he thought. He felt very sad.

The Controller waved a hand and the guards and chemists sat down. Oskar was about to sit down too when the Controller suddenly spoke. "The prisoners will remain standing."

Oskar glanced at Henrietta and caught her eye. There was something funny about the Controller's voice. What was it? The Controller spoke again. "And the rest of you will keep quiet."

Suddenly he realised. That wasn't a man's voice!

The Controller was a woman!

She flung back her black hood and stared at the three of them with pale greenish-yellow eyes like marbles. Oskar felt the Khone stir nervously beside him and at that moment something horrible, white, and furry shot out of the Controller's sleeve.

"Balthazzar," cooed the Controller. "Come back to Mummy immediately."

The Khone turned pale and looked at Oskar.

"Oh, no," he breathed. "It's Miss Cripplegate!"

CHAPTER TWENTY-THREE

"What's she doing *here*?" whispered Henrietta.

But the Khone didn't answer and, as Miss Cripplegate had retrieved her ferret and replaced it in her sleeve, Henrietta thought it wiser to keep quiet. Miss Cripplegate was very old now, but she was still quite recognisable, whereas the Khone had changed from a small boy into a man. It was more than likely that Miss Cripplegate had no idea who he was.

Miss Cripplegate sat up very straight in her ebony chair. Now and again, she slipped a gloved hand into her sleeve to stroke her ferret. Her face was dead white, waxy, and thin and at the end of her long nose hung a small bead of sweat. Oskar was wondering how she could be hot in the coldest place in the world, when she began to speak.

"As you know," she said, "my public appearances are rare. This is due to three things. One is my own great age, the next is my concern for my little treasure Balthazzar, who himself is over a hundred and twenty in ferret years. (This I ascribe to his diet of pure, fresh icecream.) The third is that for the last few years I have been devoting myself exclusively to the invention of hitherto-unknown icecream flavours."

She paused and looked around. At once, the guards and chemists began to clap. For several minutes she allowed the clapping to continue, then she went on, "At last, I perfected my flavouring process with help from my team of dedicated chemists . . ." here she inclined her head graciously to the seven of them . . . "and I judged the moment ready to launch my master plan. This plan was simple. With help from paid agents, I gradually bought up most of the world's icecream but, first, I arranged to implant a bitter tasting ingredient in certain batches from numerous icecream factories. This slowed down new production: many factory owners were ruined. Then, I had my agents steal all the remaining icecream and fly it to the Himalayas.

"Here I built my dream palace, a glittering monument to world power, for now I have come to the peak of my achievements and I intend to take over the world."

"But how?" cried Henrietta.

"I am not accustomed to being interrupted," said Miss Cripplegate coldly, "and especially not by monkeys. However, I shall tell you."

"She's mad," thought Oskar. "Totally, utterly mad and here we are at her mercy." It was not a very pleasant thought.

"Icecream has now become difficult, if not impossible, to buy," continued Miss Cripplegate. "In a few more months it will be a remembered rarity, a delicacy. People will queue up to buy it in the shops and only I, Cripplegate the Controller, will be selling it. The public will flock to buy it, they will take it home, eat it and die. My icecream will not be suspected of causing the deaths and I shall generously offer free icecream to the survivors. Naturally, they will accept and we shall be left with a handful of people whom we shall turn into slaves."

"But *of course* your icecream will be suspected," broke in Oskar.

Miss Cripplegate smiled to reveal a row of yellowish tombstone teeth.

"Little boys should be seen and not heard," she announced, "especially when they are *wrong*. After many years, I have found the secret of flavouring icecream with an agent which later disappears, leaving no trace. Foolproof! For when the icecream is tested, it will show nothing abnormal."

"But that's terrible," said the Khone. "What is this secret ingredient?"

"I have no intention of telling you," said Miss Cripplegate. "And it's not terrible but wonderful. The realisation of a lifetime's dream. If at first you don't succeed, try, try again. We have had only one problem and that is that the secret ingredient is black. Therefore the icecream must also be black."

"But people won't buy black icecream," said the Khone.

"They will if there's no other sort," said Miss Cripplegate. "And in order to make the flavour and the colour match in the icecream – for I am a perfectionist and an artist – I have had my chemists devote all their time to inventing black icecream flavours."

She gestured with her sleeve and the ferret's nose peeped out. The Khone started involuntarily. "Look around you," she went on. "Fly icecream. And we have pepper, soot, ink and belladonna."

"Belladonna!" cried the Khone, aghast. "But that's deadly nightshade. It's poisonous."

"Exactly," purred Miss Cripplegate, "and in just a moment, my dear Khone, we shall all watch you eat it."

CHAPTER TWENTY-FOUR

Miss Cripplegate's eyes narrowed. "My guards brought you to this palace," she said, "where I ordered you to be provided with all you needed, and with an unpardonable lack of gratitude, you chose to try to run away. I have a very forgiving nature, I have a soft and pliable personality, but even I cannot overlook such transgressions.

"I must punish you, but I do not wish to be unfair so I have decided to give you a sporting chance. You will be presented with a dish of black icecream and one after another you must take turns to sample it. There are three different flavours in the dish – ink, soot and belladonna, the deadly nightshade. It is impossible, except by taste, to tell which icecream is which, and to be even fairer you will draw lots for turns."

A guard stepped forward and Henrietta, Oskar and the Khone each took a straw. Oskar's was the longest, the Khone's of middling length and Henrietta drew the short straw.

"Little boy, you will go first," said Miss Cripplegate. "And remember, more haste less speed, and what's done can't be undone."

"It's her all right," said the Khone gloomily.

"And now," continued Miss Cripplegate, "let us proceed with the icecream tasting."

At a signal, a guard picked up the tray she had brought in, placed it on a small table in front of Oskar and lifted the cover to reveal a large dish of black icecream and three spoons.

Oskar gazed miserably at the dish. He had never seen icecream that looked less inviting. It was impossible to tell where one flavour began and another ended. Which part contained the deadly nightshade?

"Hurry up, little wretch!" said Miss Cripplegate. "Take your choice!"

Oskar bent forward uncertainly towards the dish.

"I . . . I . . . I don't want to," he stammered.

" 'WANT TO!' " cried Miss Cripplegate. " 'Want to' is nothing to do with it. You must and you will or the guards will either throw you to the snow leopard or lock you in the dreaded white punishment cell. This way, at least you have a chance."

Oskar stretched his hand forward and picked up the spoon. Very, very slowly, he lifted it up and dipped it into the dish. Miss Cripplegate sat watching him: the guards were totally silent. Oskar looked around the black-walled room and thought it might be the last time he would ever look at anything.

"I could even have stayed at home with Uncle Gilbert," he thought. "Whyever did I want to bring the ice-pick?"

"Hurry up!" snapped Miss Cripplegate. Oskar dug the spoon into the icecream and lifted it cautiously up towards his mouth. Miss Cripplegate leaned across the table, contorted her face into another hideous smile and hissed,

"Even I, little boy, even I, Cripplegate the Controller, the Clever, the Cosmic, the Creator, even *I* do not know which icecream is which. I have had my Chief Chemist arrange them at random in the laboratory. So even I do not yet know whether you have made a wise choice. Quickly! Eat it!"

And Oskar, closing his eyes, put the spoon into his mouth and swallowed.

CHAPTER TWENTY-FIVE

A terrible black stickiness seized his tongue making him choke and splutter. His mouth felt like the inside of a chimney. The taste was terrible and he fought to get his breath.

"Oskar!" screamed Henrietta. "Oskar, are you all right? Help, someone!"

"Control that ridiculous monkey," cried Miss Cripplegate and a guard rushed over to Henrietta and clapped his hand over her mouth. Oskar felt his breath coming in short gasps. It was as though his throat had been packed with fine dust.

Suddenly, he realised that Miss Cripplegate was looking at him with a mixture of fury and disappointment. Happiness overwhelmed him. Of course! It tasted of soot! And if it was soot icecream then it couldn't be belladonna. He was still alive.

"Too clever by half!" snarled Miss Cripplegate. "Move the tray."

The guard placed it in front of the Khone.

"You must choose yours at least a spoon's width on either side of where your friend has dug," said Miss Cripplegate. "Of course it gives you less choice, but should you be fortunate enough to choose the ink, then your little talking monkey friend will be forced to choose the nightshade. One of you will certainly entertain us by dying in agony very shortly."

The Khone picked up his spoon with trembling fingers. Bravely, he raised it and dug into the dish. Just as he lifted the

spoon to his lips, there came a loud hammering at the door and two guards burst in.

"Emergency!" they shouted. "The yetis are attacking the palace!"

The room broke out in uproar. Miss Cripplegate rose to her feet.

"SILENCE!" she thundered. "AT ONCE! The situation is *not* urgent. The yetis are unarmed. Detachments of guards, secure the windows and the service doors, and a double detachment secure the front of the palace. Do your duty and return immediately. And you," she said blisteringly to the guards who had raised the alarm, "are confined to the dungeons for seven days. Did your mothers never teach you manners? To burst into a closed room without knocking! What impudence! What impertinence! HOW DARE YOU?"

"But Controller," pleaded one of them, "it's an emergency!"

"Emergency?" Miss Cripplegate was outraged. "How DARE

you decide what constitutes an emergency? This is *my* castle and *my* empire. I decide, and no one else, whether or not we have an emergency on our hands."

"Controller," put in the other guard, "it *seems* like an emergency. There are hordes of them approaching. It's like watching a tornado of snow heading towards us."

"Rubbish!" snapped Miss Cripplegate. "The yetis are unarmed and this palace is impregnable."

The Chief Chemist leaned forward.

"It may," he suggested, "be prudent to return the yeti baby you captured with the gorilla. Perhaps they want the baby and maybe it would be as well to give them the gorilla too. It's been nothing but trouble since we captured it. I understand several of the guards have been bitten quite severely."

"Return the gorilla to the yetis. Unthinkable!" cried Miss Cripplegate. "And I shall keep the yeti baby until is a little older then have it skinned for dear Balthazzar to sleep on."

The Chief Chemist leaned back. "As you wish, Controller," he said.

Miss Cripplegate looked at the Khone. "You appear to have gained a little time from this interruption," she said, "but remember, a bird in the hand is worth two in the bush. Soon, the guards will return and we shall resume where we left off."

Try as he might, the Khone could not see any difference in colour or texture in the icecream in front of him. Beside him, Henrietta was hoping desperately that the yetis might reach the windows and doors before the guards, and storm the palace. These hopeful thoughts were wiped out by the reappearance of the guards. "We were rather longer, Controller," said their spokesman, "because we waited to see what the yetis would do."

"Very wise. I commend you," said Miss Cripplegate. "And?"

"They were unable to break down the doors or burst through in any way. We are totally secure, Controller."

"As I thought," purred Miss Cripplegate. "Sit down again and we shall carry on."

She turned to the Khone. "You have had an exceptionally long time to make your choice," she said, "and therefore we shall wait no longer. He who hesitates is lost. Begin *now*!"

The Khone looked pale and confused. He dug his spoon into the dish, lifted it to his lips and paused.

There was no sound inside the room but, from outside, came a muffled grunting and shouting. The Khone continued to clutch his spoon in mid-air. Miss Cripplegate inclined her head.

"The fury of disappointment," she murmured. "Dumb animals have not the brains of noble men or women. You hear outside the frustrated cries of the lesser beasts."

There came a thud. Oskar and Henrietta looked up. Above and behind Miss Cripplegate's head, a crack appeared in the wall. There was another muffled thud and the crack widened. Oskar gazed upwards. Again there was a thud and this time, as the crack became a large split, he could see through to the outside. There stood the yeti queen with hordes of yetis behind her. She had something raised high above her head, ready for the final blow that would allow the wall to open enough to let the yetis pour through. Oskar peered intently: he thought he recognised it.

And just at that moment, Henrietta, beside him, jumped to her feet and shouted wildly, "Oskar! Oskar! Look what she's using to break down the wall! It's the ice-pick!!"

CHAPTER TWENTY-SIX

Miss Cripplegate had remained transfixed during the thuds and blows but now she seemed to regain her senses.

"Rally!" she ordered. "Rally! Guards assemble and defend the palace!"

The guards looked nervously at the yeti queen outlined in the gap in the wall. She brought down the ice-pick with a crash, a huge chunk of the wall crumbled under the impact and, screaming and chattering, she leapt through the gap and straight at Miss Cripplegate! The Chief Chemist jumped up and, closely followed by the rest of the chemists and most of the guards, raced out of the room with dozens of yetis in hot pursuit.

The queen seized Miss Cripplegate by the throat and as she did so, the ferret escaped from one dangling black sleeve and ran eagerly towards the dish of icecream.

"No, Balthazzar! No! *No*! NO!" screamed Miss Cripplegate as she tried frantically to break away.

Balthazzar stopped at the dish, sniffed the icecream, then gobbled up every bit.

"Oh no!" moaned Miss Cripplegate. "Oh, my darling Balthazzar! What have you done?"

The ferret which had been polishing off the plate with a final lick, stopped for a moment, then suddenly began to writhe in agony on the floor. For a few moments it thrashed and jerked

about, squeaking piteously, then it gave a final shudder and lay
still.

Oskar watched as its eyes glazed over, then turned to look at
Miss Cripplegate. She was sitting motionless in the yeti's grasp,
staring at Balthazzar and, as Oskar watched, he saw tears come
to her eyes and slowly trickle down her cheeks.

"Henrietta," he whispered, awestruck. "Look! Miss Cripplegate's crying and even her tears are black."

And it was true. Pale black water oozed from her eyes and
ran down her chalk white cheeks. Oskar felt suddenly sorry for
her.

"She must feel awful," he said to Henrietta.

"I don't see why," said practical Henrietta. "That's exactly what she was going to do to *us*. I'm not a bit sorry for her."

As she spoke, the yeti queen, suddenly noticing her, dropped Miss Cripplegate and hugged Henrietta warmly. Then she slung her onto her back, snatched up Miss Cripplegate again and vanished out of the door.

"Hey!" called Oskar. "Come back! Where are you going?"

Everyone had disappeared. Only Oskar and the Khone remained in the room. They could hear Miss Cripplegate's receding voice calling in vain, "Guards! Chemists! Help! Help!"

"We *have* had a lucky escape," said the Khone. "To think that the Controller was Miss Cripplegate, all the time."

"What will the queen do to her?" asked Oskar.

"I'm afraid," said the Khone, "she'll probably throw Miss Cripplegate to the snow leopard that lives in the dungeon. Then she'll want to find her baby, so she and Henrietta will be searching for it. Why don't we try to find them?"

They set off along the passage and down the stairs and had not gone far when they heard an enormous amount of noise. Yetis were chattering, guards and chemists were screaming and calling out and, above the din, Oskar could hear Henrietta shouting something he couldn't quite catch. They quickened their pace until they reached the floor below where an incredible sight met them.

All the guards were tied up like parcels with the same vines that Oskar had used for his escape from the cave. Of Miss Cripplegate and the queen there was no sign, but Henrietta stood holding the yeti baby in her arms.

"We found the queen's baby!" she shouted. "The poor little

thing was in a room all by itself. And there might be more prisoners in the cells. Some of these doors are double-bolted. Hurry up and help me undo them."

"How did you find the baby so quickly?" asked Oskar.

"The queen did," said Henrietta. "She just sniffed at all the doors, stopped at one, gave a swipe with the ice-pick, broke down the door, and there was the baby inside. Then she gave it to me to hold and took off with Miss Cripplegate."

"To the snow leopard, I expect," said the Khone grimly.

Just at that moment, as if to prove his words, there came a shriek from further below them. It was followed by the sound of an animal roaring and someone screaming.

Everyone fell silent. Oskar and Henrietta shivered.

"Well, she's gone," said the Khone, "and though she was a dreadfully evil creature, I'm sorry she had to die in such a horrible way."

"She did it to other people," said Henrietta.

"True," agreed the Khone. "But it's still a nasty business. Now, let's see to these bolts and find out whether there are other prisoners in here. We certainly couldn't hear them through doors and walls as thick as these."

He drew back the bolts on the first cell and pushed the door open. There was no one inside.

"They're probably all empty," said Oskar, "but we ought to make sure."

The second cell was also empty. The Khone opened the third one and gave a gasp of surprise!

A stern, thin figure rose up from the bed and pointed an accusing finger at him.

CHAPTER TWENTY-SEVEN

"Ernest Ebenezer Barnsbury Tooks," said the figure, "I could never have believed you to have fallen into such evil ways. Release me at once!"

"He knows you!" cried Henrietta.

"Of course he knows me," said the Khone. "He's my oldest friend, Walter Wilberforce Whibley. He and I have been ice-cream manufacturers and friendly rivals for years."

"No longer," said Walter Wilberforce Whibley. "To lock up your oldest friendly rival whilst you planned to take over the world's icecream stocks, is the most despicable, wicked . . ."

"Walter, wait!" broke in the Khone. "It's not like that at all. *I've* been locked up too until a few hours ago. It's not me who's done this to you."

"It's true," said Oskar. "The Khone's been the Controller's prisoner for ages."

"I thought *you* must be the Controller," said Walter Wilberforce Whibley. "Do forgive me. But why were we locked up like this? I came on a mission to find out about the icecream thefts and was seized and incarcerated."

"My story exactly," said the Khone. "Now, Wafer, stay there. I'll unbolt the rest of the doors and then we can have a long chat. How wonderful to see you again."

"I thought you said his name was Walter, not Wafer," said Henrietta.

"It is Walter," said the Khone, "but he's always known as the Wafer — wafer-thin, you see — and I am the Khone — round and fat."

Henrietta grinned.

"I'll come with you," said the Wafer. "I'm not anxious to spend a minute longer in this cell. But I doubt whether you'll find any other prisoners. I gather that when any of the guards displeased the Controller, they were fed to the snow leopard. And, by the way, where *is* the Controller?"

"I'll tell you as we go," said the Khone and, deep in

conversation, he shot back the bolts on cell after cell.

"*We'll* push the doors open and look in," offered Henrietta.

"You just go on unbolting and talking to Wafer."

"That's a talking gorilla," said the Wafer, much impressed.

"It must be worth a fortune, Khone. Where did you find it?"

"I'm *not* an it, I'm a *her*," said Henrietta in great annoyance.

"And, of *course* I'm not a gorilla. I'm a gorillagram and this is my uniform."

"What does a gorillagram do?" asked the Wafer.

"It sings," explained Henrietta. "Like this," and she began, ♫ "La, la, la, la.

> *Don't send a card!*
> *Don't send a letter!*
> *Always remember*
> *A gorillagram is better!*

> *It shows you're very thoughtful*
> *And it doesn't cost much more*
> *To give your friends the pleasure of*
> *Gorillas at the door.*

> *What is better than a present*
> *Or a card you really like?*
> *Just the fascinating thrill of*
> *A gorilla on a bike.*

> *Don't send a letter!*
> *Don't send a card!*
> *Sending a gorillagram*
> *Really isn't hard.*

Just phone up with your message
And in half an hour or less,
We'll dispatch a trained gorilla
To the relevant address.

So don't send a card
And don't send a letter!
Simply remember –
A gorillagram is better!" ♩♪

"Very good," cried the Khone and the Wafer.

Henrietta gave a little bow. Meanwhile, Oskar was peering into the cells. They were all empty.

"There's another floor below this," said the Khone. "We should look there and check as well. One of the guards once said they sometimes kept prisoners there. 'Punishment cells' he called them. I gather they're rather uncomfortable compared with these."

The Wafer snorted. "Where *are* the guards anyway?" he asked.

"Tied up," said the Khone. "Literally. By the yetis."

They moved down to the floor below. The passage was smaller and narrower. The Khone put on the light and there, in front of them, they saw the yeti queen clutching the ice-pick. Growling, she advanced towards them.

"Quick, Henrietta!" shouted Oskar. "Give her the baby back!"

But at the sight of Henrietta, the yeti queen dropped the ice-pick, and enfolded both Henrietta and the baby in a furry hug.

"Look at that," said the Wafer. "I expect she doesn't trust humans since Miss Cripplegate stole her baby."

"If I kiss you one after the other," said Henrietta through a mouthful of shaggy fur, "she might kiss you, too, and realise you're friends."

"Good idea," said the Wafer.

Oskar was not too sure about being kissed by a yeti or even Henrietta for that matter, but her idea did make sense. She wriggled away from the yeti, and kissed them one after the other. The yeti queen, with great lipsmacking noises, followed suit. First the Khone, then the Wafer, then it was Oskar's turn and he felt a great curtain of white shaggy fur sweep over him and a warm rubbery kiss on his cheek.

"It worked!" said Henrietta. "Now let's look quickly in these rooms and make sure they're all empty. Khone and Wafer, you unbolt the doors and Oskar and I will check the cells. Then we can go back upstairs."

The Khone unbolted the first door and Oskar looked inside. Empty! The Wafer unbolted the second door and Henrietta, peering in, gave a squeak of excitement. "There *is* someone here. There's a man chained to the wall."

But Oskar, who had just opened the third door, didn't hear her. There was someone in his cell, too. Asleep on a bed, with a long chain attached to one ankle, lay a dishevelled figure.

Oskar's heart beat faster. He crept out into the hall and picked up the ice-pick. The others had crowded into the second cell and didn't notice him. All the better. He carried the pick into the cell, set it beside the table, then leaned over and shook the sleeping figure.

"Wake up!" he called. "Wake up, Mum! It's me. Oskar! I've brought you your ice-pick!"

CHAPTER TWENTY-EIGHT

"OSKAR!" cried his mother. "Am I dreaming?" And she showered him with kisses. "And you *have* got the ice-pick," she said. "But how on earth did you get here? I've been in this frightful prison since just after I sent the telegram. Why, what's the matter?"

For Oskar was crying.

"Oh, Mum," he wept, "I thought you were dead. We found your anorak and it was all bloodstained and I was so cross with you."

"Well, you can stop being cross with me now you've found I'm still alive," said his mother and she hugged him tightly. Oskar cuddled close to her.

"I didn't want you to be dead," he said.

"Of course you didn't," said his mother, and she wiped his face dry with the end of the blanket. "It must have been terrible for you. Why don't you tell me all about it?"

Oskar was deep into the story when Henrietta appeared at the door.

"What do you think?" she began excitedly. "The man next door is *another* icecream manufacturer! He's called . . . Oh!" She broke off as she took in Oskar's mother.

Cornelia went to get up but the chain stopped her. She looked at Henrietta's gorilla suit.

"You must be Henrietta," she said. "Oskar's just been telling me what happened."

"We'll have to get that chain off," said Oskar.

"It won't pull off," said Henrietta. "We tried already next door. But hold on a moment." And she bustled out. Two minutes later she returned with the yeti queen ambling beside her. Oskar's mother shrank back in horror.

"What's that?" she gasped.

"A yeti queen," said Henrietta. "And she's adopted me. She thinks I'm a gorilla."

"I can see why," said Cornelia. "You do seem rather at home in that suit."

"Watch this," said Henrietta and she bent down and showed the chain to the yeti.

"But it *can't* be a yeti," said Cornelia, "because yetis don't exist."

"They do!" cried Oskar. "I haven't told you that bit yet, but we've been in their cave. *And* been carried over the snow by them."

The yeti queen picked up the chain, snapped it cleanly in two then, reaching round Cornelia's ankle, carefully broke the shackle.

"Gosh, she's strong," said Oskar.

His mother noticed the baby clinging to the queen's back.

"What a lovely little baby one," she said, and reached out to stroke it. Like a flash, the yeti bared her teeth and snarled at Cornelia.

"She doesn't trust humans," said Henrietta, "because Miss Cripplegate stole her baby. She was going to kill it later on."

"It's all right," said Oskar, "Henrietta knows how to make her friendly. Go on, Henrietta."

Henrietta kissed Oskar's mother on the cheek and the yeti did the same.

"You're safe, now," said Henrietta. Cornelia stood up and put her arm round Oskar.

"It feels unreal," she said. "I can't believe I'm free. Let's get out of here and join your other friends."

"Mum," said Oskar, "I'm so glad we've found you."

And they set off down the passage.

CHAPTER TWENTY-NINE

Next day, Oskar, Henrietta, Cornelia, the Khone and the Wafer went on a skiing picnic to a lake in a valley on the other side of the palace. Henrietta had been reluctant to go, partly because she was now wearing only her long white thermal underwear.

"We've found skis in one of the palace cupboards," said Cornelia. "And the lake's really pretty, Henrietta. You'll love it."

"What about my clothes?" demanded Henrietta.

"I'll lend you my anorak," said Cornelia, 'and if you wear that over your thermal underwear suit, it will hardly show at all."

"I wish I still had my gorilla suit," complained Henrietta.

She was being extremely difficult. At first she had been nice to Oskar's mother, but she'd got more and more unpleasant as the day wore on, and the gorilla suit had been the final straw.

"I know you're upset about not having your gorilla suit," said Cornelia, "but as soon as we get back home, I'll get you another one. I promise."

"What'll I wear at home until you do?" asked Henrietta.

"Some of your other clothes, of course," said Cornelia.

"I haven't *got* any other clothes," said Henrietta sulkily. "And, anyway, I *like* my gorilla suit."

"There wasn't any choice," said Cornelia, getting rather cross. "Did you want to have to live with the yetis for the rest of your life?"

"Yes, as a matter of fact," said Henrietta and stalked off.

For, after they had freed her, Oskar's mother had tried to sort out what to do next. The main problem had been the yeti queen who kept picking up Henrietta and carrying her around. Henrietta was pleased by this attention but it worried Cornelia.

"The queen may take her off," she said, "and then it would be impossible to find her. We'd have very little chance of getting her back if the yeti queen didn't want us to. We must do something."

They all thought hard for some time. Then Oskar had an idea. "They love Henrietta because they think she's another monkey," he said. "And it can't be because she *smells* like a monkey, because she doesn't."

Henrietta was deeply offended.

"So," Oskar went on, "it must be because she *looks* like a monkey, and if she takes her gorilla suit off and we stuff it with blankets, we can give it to the yetis and they can keep it!"

Cornelia felt this was an excellent idea so Henrietta got out of her suit and they padded it and put it in the passageway.

"It won't work," said Henrietta. "She'll know it's not me."

But the queen rushed up to the dummy and hugged it. It fell over and she seemed upset. She shook it and kissed it and finally, clutching it against her, she vanished upstairs. She took no notice at all of the real Henrietta who was standing watching in her white thermal underwear suit.

Some time later, the Khone, who had been looking round upstairs, came running to Oskar. "Quick!" he gasped. "The yetis have left with Henrietta. They've all taken off across the snow. We must hurry!"

"Don't worry," said Oskar. "Here's Henrietta. The yetis only took her gorilla suit stuffed with blankets."

The Khone looked hard at Henrietta.

"Good gracious," he said. "I would never have recognised you."

Henrietta stood feeling foolish in her long white underwear. No one else had any spare clothes to lend her and she felt cross and ill-used. She wished she had gone with the yetis: it would have been nice to have been a queen and to have had everybody doing what she wanted. On the other hand, remembering the dried meat and the snow and the terrifying leap over the precipice, she decided maybe it wouldn't have been so good after all.

So the next morning, to cheer Henrietta up, Cornelia had suggested the picnic, and they had all come down to the lake on skis. The sun was out and it was warmer. After lunch, the others had decided to have a rest by the water, but Oskar and Henrietta had thought it would be fun to explore a bit and Cornelia had agreed they could go to the river alone.

The snow stopped near the top of the valley where they'd left their skis, and, from the snowline to the lake, the ground was covered with grass and small alpine flowers.

"See those flowers," said Henrietta. "They're the same as the ones the yetis brought to the cave. I wonder if this is where they got them."

"Let's take some back to Mum," said Oskar. So they picked several bunches of pink and white flowers, then walked on further.

"I can see the river!" cried Henrietta.

"Mum said it goes all the way down through India to the sea," said Oskar, "but it doesn't look very big."

"It's deep though," said Henrietta, "so we'd better not fall in."

"What have the Khone and the Wafer decided to do?" asked Oskar, as they walked towards the river.

"At first, they were going to demolish the palace," said Henrietta, "but they've changed their minds. Now they're going to run it together as an icecream-inventing laboratory. They're going to let the chemists and the guards keep working there on new icecream inventions that won't harm people."

"What are they going to do with Miss Cripplegate's black icecream?" asked Oskar.

"They've melted it already," said Henrietta, "and made the Chief Chemist burn the formula. Hey! Look over there! There's something in the river!"

"Where?" said Oskar. "I can't see anything."

"Over there!" said Henrietta. "It's moving."

Oskar stared.

Slowly, slowly, up the river, struggling against the current, a strangely familiar figure was swimming. It was wearing a black wetsuit and an aqualung.

"It's Elspeth!" shrieked Oskar. "Elspeth! Elspeth! It's me! Oskar!"

CHAPTER THIRTY

The swimmer lifted her head out of the water and looked up.

"Good heavens!" she cried. "This can't be true!" And she swam to the bank and climbed out. "It *is* you, Oskar, darling, but whatever are you doing here in South America?"

"I'm not in South America," said Oskar. "I'm in the Himalayas, and so are you."

Elspeth was amazed. "Are you sure?"

"Of course I'm sure," said Oskar.

"Well, it does explain the snow everywhere. I thought it was rather strange."

"But what are you *doing* here?" asked Oskar.

'I'm swimming my lap of honour," explained Elspeth. "I won the Grandmothers' Underwater Cross-Atlantic Race and I've got a wonderful medal and I'm terribly famous. The Americans wanted to fly me home on Concorde but I said I'd swim the round trip just to show everyone I could do it. Only, somehow, I got lost. Then I met a charming school of porpoises who escorted me up to the tip of South America. I've been swimming ever since, but I must have lost my bearings again. And why are you still in the Himalayas?"

"Because of all sorts of things," said Oskar. "We've been in prison in a palace – me and Henrietta – that's the telegram gorilla – *and* Mum – but we didn't know she . . ."

"Oskar," said Elspeth, "this aqualung is very heavy and I'm

a trifle hungry, so do you think we could go and get some food somewhere, and then could you tell me all about it?"

"But what have you been eating, Elspeth, if you've been in the sea all the time?"

"Plankton, darling," sighed his grandmother. "And although plankton's terribly nutritious, it doesn't quite have the *substance* of ordinary food. So if there's anything to eat nearby, I would be rather pleased to find it."

"Of course we'll find you something," said Oskar, "and I am glad you won." He gave her a big kiss. "Aren't you cold? You've only got your rubber suit on."

"Dear me, no," said Elspeth. "This suit is insulated. I'm quite, quite snug inside it."

Oskar wanted to race over the snow, shouting and calling the news to his mother, but Elspeth's aqualung forced them to walk quite slowly and he didn't feel he could leave her with Henrietta and run on ahead.

"You haven't introduced me to your friend, Oskar," said Elspeth.

"You've met her already," said Oskar. "She's the telegram gorilla and her name's Henrietta."

"Well, Henrietta," said Elspeth, "I really have to say that the Post Office has made a mistake. Your gorilla suit did a lot more for you than that dreadful set of white underwear you've got on now."

"I don't *have* my gorilla suit any more," cried Henrietta, stung. "I can't go round with nothing on and nobody's got any other clothes for me."

"How very fortunate," said Elspeth, "that I packed my tutu. It's in that little waterproof bag of luggage under my aqualung. There was a gala concert after the race and, as I expected, people *insisted* that I dance for them. Just in case, I'd packed my tutu and my ballet shoes, so I was able to give them a short solo from Swan Lake. Naturally, they were rapturous. I suggest you put the tutu on later, Henrietta, and cover that dreadful underwear. With a tutu over the top you'll look quite presentable."

"Is it a real tutu?" asked Henrietta.

"Of course it's a real one," said Elspeth. "I've worn it in some extremely famous performances and you're fortunate that my generosity exceeds my sentimentality."

Henrietta was not quite sure what this meant, but feeling that wearing a tutu was certainly preferable to wearing only the thermal underwear, she said nothing.

"What happened when you won, Elspeth?" asked Oskar.

Elspeth sighed. "Rather a busy time," she replied. "Masses of parties, interviews everywhere, tickertape welcomes, hundreds of invitations and I was absolutely lionised all the time wherever I went. Terribly boring, really. I had to *insist* on fitting in my daily aqualung practice. As a matter of fact, one of my prizes is a new gold-plated bucket."

"What are your other prizes?" asked Oskar.

"I can't keep track," said Elspeth airily. "They've been simply pouring in all the time. An aquarium of tropical fish, a motorbike, a holiday in Japan, a year's supply of spaghetti bolognaise, six medals, four gerbils, a burglar alarm, a gold watch, and a white rhino which will have to stay in the zoo." She broke off. "We must be nearly there," she said.

"Almost," said Henrietta. "But I've got an idea. Do you remember the telegram I was supposed to deliver for your mother, Oskar?" He nodded. "Well, I never sang it because we couldn't find her. But how about this instead?"

She cleared her throat and began.

♪♪ "La, la, la, la,

> *Look behind me*
> *When I've sung,*
> *There's Elspeth*
> *In her aqualung."* ♪♪

She raced away from them over the snow and panted up to Cornelia and the others.

"I'm a hairless singing yetigram!" she announced and began to sing.

When she had finished, Cornelia looked up.

"Good heavens!" she said, "it *is* Mother. I thought you and Oskar were having a joke." She got up, ran over to Elspeth and kissed her. "But, Mother," she said, "how do you come to be here?"

"A simple case of geographical misdirection," explained Elspeth, "and, Cornelia, you know how much I dislike being called Mother. It's terribly aging."

"Sorry, Elspeth," said Cornelia.

"I realise this may sound rather rude," said Elspeth faintly, "but I am exceedingly hungry and I *would* appreciate a morsel or two of food."

"Sit down Mo . . . Elspeth," said Cornelia, "and we'll find you something immediately."

"Oskar's been telling me what happened," went on Elspeth, "and I do hope you've finally got the ice-pick. Ah, thank you for the sandwich. Now, while I eat it, can someone please unstrap my luggage, take out my tutu and cover that child's frightful underwear suit?"

The Wafer got up, pulled out the tutu and passed it to Henrietta.

"Here you are," he said. Henrietta put it on, and did a few steps in the snow.

"Infinitely better," commented Elspeth, "and yes, thank you, I shall have another sandwich."

"As soon as you're ready, Elspeth," said Cornelia, "we'll all go back to the palace and you can snuggle into a nice warm bed."

"Good Lord, no!" cried Elspeth. "I'm sorry, but it's out of the question. I'm simply stopping off for this little family picnic and then I must get straight back into the river and carry on with my round-the-world lap of honour."

Cornelia was annoyed. "Don't be ridiculous, Mother."

"There's nothing ridiculous about it at all," said Elspeth calmly. "I shall simply ask you to point me in the right direction and carry on from where I left off. And don't argue. My mind is quite made up."

"You were going upstream," the Wafer pointed out, "but if you turned around and headed downstream, you would fairly soon get down into the Ganges and from there straight out into the Indian Ocean."

"Ah, the Ganges," said Elspeth. "Of course, I must already have come *up* it on my way here. Rather a lot of fires on the bank at one point, I remember, and it's very wide lower down. Now the Indian Ocean's no problem at all. I simply cross it, get into the Red Sea, up the Suez Canal, across the Mediterranean, through the Straits of Gibraltar, over the Bay of Biscay and up the Channel and home. It wouldn't surprise me at all, Cornelia, if I arrived home before you and Oskar. Right, I must be off. Thank you for the sandwiches."

She stood up, kissed Oskar and Cornelia, shook hands with the others and set off back to the river.

"And take care of that tutu, please," she called over her shoulder to Henrietta, as they waved her goodbye.

"I think we'd better get back now," said Cornelia and they packed their things and set off to collect their skis and return to the palace.

CHAPTER THIRTY-ONE

It was a week later. Oskar, Henrietta, and Cornelia were saying goodbye to the Khone and the Wafer before flying home in a private helicopter.

"A private helicopter! How very impressive!" said the Khone.

"It's one of Elspeth's prizes," explained Oskar. "She telephoned the pilot to collect us here."

"She TELEPHONED?" cried the Wafer. "How could she have telephoned when she's in the ocean?"

"She's got a portable waterproof telephone in her pack," said Oskar.

"Yes," said Henrietta, with a giggle, and she imitated Elspeth perfectly. "She said, 'Oskar, darling, I wouldn't *consider* racing without a telephone. Why, I might be asked to swim in another competition and miss the invitation altogether if I wasn't available'."

Everybody laughed, they all kissed and hugged goodbye and then climbed aboard.

"Come back and visit us!" called the Wafer.

The rotor blades began to whirr.

"We're lifting off," warned the pilot. They pressed their noses to the windows and waved as the Khone and the Wafer became smaller and smaller and finally faded away into tiny dots below them. Then they settled back into their seats.

"Henrietta," asked Cornelia, "who will be meeting you at the airport?"

"No one," said Henrietta. "But it's all right. I left my bicycle chained up in the left luggage deposit."

"I shall ring your parents as soon as we arrive," said Cornelia. "They must be awfully worried by now."

Henrietta glared at Cornelia.

"She doesn't have any parents," Oskar broke in. "She lives by herself."

"Nonsense," said Cornelia. "She can't possibly live by herself. She's still a child. It's against the law."

"Too bad," said Henrietta. "I do live by myself and I'm going to go on like that."

"But who cooks your meals?"

"I do," said Henrietta. "And I clean my room and make my bed and everything."

"That's very impressive," said Cornelia slowly, "and I'm sure you do it well, but don't you ever get lonely?"

"Never!" said Henrietta.

"How about Christmas?" asked Cornelia. Henrietta said nothing. "Or your birthday?" she persisted. Henrietta hung her head.

"When is your birthday?" asked Oskar.

Henrietta stared even harder at the floor of the helicopter.

"Tomorrow," she muttered.

"*Tomorrow!*" cried Cornelia. "Why, we must have a party."

"I don't *want* a party," said Henrietta nastily and she burst into tears. "It's no good wanting any parents or a family, if you're as old as me," she wept. "I'm eleven years old. Nobody wants to adopt an older child. I'd just have to go into a Home."

Cornelia looked very hard at Oskar. He nodded.

"Henrietta," said Cornelia, "I was wondering if you'd like to come and live with Oskar and me. We've got very fond of you, and in a way you'd be doing us a favour because Oskar gets lonely and fed up when I go away on expeditions." She looked at Oskar again and went on, "Now he's shown me how well he coped with the ice-pick, of course, he'll have to come on expeditions in the holidays, but in term time, he'll still have to stay behind."

"Wow! Hurray!" yelled Oskar, leaping out of his seat and dancing round the cabin. "Go on, Henrietta, say 'Yes!'."

Henrietta looked at Cornelia for a moment, then she said, "Would I really be doing you a favour?"

"Definitely," said Cornelia.

"Can I still keep my room?"

"No," said Cornelia, "because we can't afford it, and you

can't go on being a gorillagram because you'll have to go to school."

"You promised me a new gorilla suit," said Henrietta.

"And I'll get it for you," said Cornelia, "but you can't go on being a gorillagram."

"School's not bad," said Oskar. "I quite like it."

"Well, think it over," offered Cornelia.

"I don't want to think it over, thank you," said Henrietta. "You might change your mind. I'll come." She fingered her tutu. "Do you think Elspeth will let me keep this?"

"Probably not that one," said Cornelia. "But certainly one of her other ones."

"I wouldn't mind not being a gorillagram if I had a tutu," said Henrietta.

"And a mother," said Oskar.

"Cornelia's not my mother," said Henrietta. "She's yours."

Cornelia smiled at her. "If I adopted you I'd be your mother," she said.

Henrietta looked at Cornelia and grinned. "Then Oskar would be my brother," she said and she started to jump and sing too.

"It's getting a bit noisy back there," called the pilot.

"Sorry," said Cornelia. "Now you two be quiet and get some sleep."

Some time later, they were woken by the pilot.

"Take a look below!" he called. "We're almost there!"

Beneath them was the Thames and on one bank stood a crowd of people carrying flags and banners. The pilot indicated the jetty beside the water.

"That's where we're going to land," he shouted.

Down, down, down they came. The ground came zooming up towards them and with a bump they landed. Through the windows, they could hear the noise of the crowd.

"But why are they all there?" asked Oskar.

"To welcome you back, of course," said the pilot. "Read the banners!"

"Us?" cried Henrietta and Oskar together and they craned to see what the writing said.

ICECREAM HEROES WELCOME! read one, and THANK YOU, OSKAR AND HENRIETTA! said another. There were dozens of them. Oskar could see

HAIL HIMALAYAN HEROES!!
A WORLD SAFE FOR ICECREAM!
ICECREAM FREAKS UNITED
I LICK ICECREAM
and GREETINGS FROM THE GRATEFUL GROCERS

"It wasn't really us who saved the icecream. It was the yetis," said Henrietta.

"I think," said Cornelia, "it would be much kinder and fairer to the yetis, not to mention them at all. They don't want humans hunting them as trophies. It's much better for you to take the credit and leave the yetis their privacy. Besides, if it hadn't been for Henrietta, the yetis wouldn't have gone to the palace anyway."

"I suppose so," agreed Henrietta, and Oskar nodded.

"They've seen you!" shouted the pilot. "Listen!"

The cheering of the crowd became a roar as people glimpsed

their faces through the windows. Then, suddenly, as if by magic, all the heads turned in the opposite direction.

"Something's happening on the river," said the pilot. "I'll just turn on the intercom and see if I can pick up a message."

He flicked a switch and the cabin was filled with static. Through the noisy blur, a familiar voice could be heard.

"Absolutely *perfect* timing, Cornelia, dear. I was just racing up the Thames when I saw the chopper coming down. Marvellous."

"But, Mother," shouted Cornelia into the intercom, "how have you got here so quickly?"

"That delightful school of porpoises found me *again*," crackled Elspeth's voice, "and insisted on escorting me and carrying me on their backs. I've simply *flown*. As soon as you get out of the helicopter, I'll meet you on the jetty."

"By the way, Mother. . . ."

"Elspeth!" interrupted Elspeth.

"Sorry . . . Elspeth," went on Cornelia. "I've decided to adopt Henrietta."

"Excellent!" said Elspeth. "I shall teach her my tap dance routine. Now hurry up, please. I don't want to have to linger around in the Thames waiting for you."

The pilot flung open the door.

Oskar and Henrietta stood on the steps with Cornelia behind them and watched the crowd surging and waving.

Cornelia put one arm round Oskar and the other round Henrietta and hugged them both tightly. "Do you know, I'm really glad I forgot my ice-pick," she said.

Over the intercom came Elspeth's voice loud and clear, "I'd just like to remind you, Cornelia, that sending Oskar with the ice-pick was actually *my* idea."

"Oh, Elspeth," said Oskar. "It wasn't! It was *mine*!"

"Well, whosever it was, it was a wonderful idea," said Cornelia. "And could you carry it now, please, Oskar? I've got too much luggage already."

"All right," said Oskar.

"I'll help you," said Henrietta.

And they set off together down the steps towards the waiting crowd.

THE END